Sapphire Guardians Book 1

A Crimson Moon Hideaway Novel

Cherron Riser

Cherish the Fallen
Cherron Riser
A Crimson Moon Hideaway Novel
Copyright ©2021
Edited by: Kelly Hartigan (XterraWeb)
Published by: Celtic Hearts Press, LLC
Cover by: A Beautiful Mess Designs
Formatting by: Celtic Hearts Press, LLC

Dedication

A special thank you to Kerrin. I appreciate all your support and assistance in helping me grow. You have helped me find my strength and belief once again.

Also, to my guardian angel wherever you may be. Thank you for always looking out for me.

Chapter 1

Lyla

"What do you mean I have to take a vacation? There is nothing wrong," Lyla nearly whined when she saw the correspondence Kristoph had brought to her. People said not to kill the messenger, but she was not happy with the news. However, she wasn't tempted to kill him; it simply wasn't in her nature.

"I am just here to deliver what came down from the boss." Kristoph was already backing out of the room as he spoke. "It doesn't hurt to take time off. Seriously. You could use it."

Lyla didn't want a vacation. Nothing in her life made her happier than the work she did, and the idea of taking time off and away from her children was a bit daunting to her. Who was going to look after them while she was away? What happened if they were hurt, and she wasn't able to get to them? Of course, that was a bit ridiculous considering she had the ability to get to them at a moment's notice from anywhere in the world; it was part of the gifts of her people. It didn't mean she felt comfortable with it.

"Look, can you let him know that I appreciate his concern, but I'm fine and just want to continue doing my normal duties." Lyla turned to find she was talking to an empty room. Well then, how was that supposed to help anything? Frustrated, she stomped her foot and tossed the letter down on the bed in her room. She didn't leave it there for very long. Something about things being out of place bothered her. She quickly picked up the notice and placed it on the corner of her desk where the rest of her mail had been neatly stacked.

Most of her friends had collections of things decorating their rooms, but Lyla was simple and clean. Her room showed that. Her bed was made, adorned with white bedding and crisp lines. It was the kind of bed you could bounce a quarter off. Her desk was neatly organized in sections— mail, orders, and dossiers on her current charges. A small organizer had pens and other office supplies that were also perfectly placed without a single thing off from where it should be. Her dresser was clear of clutter and filled with her normal white clothing, perfectly pressed and folded before being stacked in proper rows inside the drawers, and her closet was organized by the purpose of the dress. All in all, it was a sterile, boring space where she stayed when she wasn't working.

which means we are going to go and do something fun, and I'm not going to make you do it alone. Now, perk up. You are long past due having some you time."

"Yeah, me time." Lyla smiled and shook her head. Like she knew what to do with all this. "So, I take it you have something in mind."

"You know I do." Zimarra nearly vibrated with her sudden burst of laughter.

"Hey now, no getting me into trouble. I know you, and I don't want to get myself into any kind of mess like you." Lyla felt more lighthearted the more she talked with her friend.

They had been together since the beginning, training as guardian angels and even going on their first missions together. For centuries, they worked together until the time came for them to go out on their own, but that didn't stop them from being the best of friends. However, unlike Lyla, Zimarra was never afraid to be adventurous. Which at times led the mischievous girl into some peculiar situations. Nothing worthy of the fall, but still. Zimarra had never feared skirting that line, and Lyla was not sure she was willing to do the same.

"I am not going to lead you to do anything you don't want to do. I just want you to have a good time. Look." Zimarra held out a pamphlet with information about a hotel and spa. The picture on the front featured a gorgeous resort nestled in a thick redwood forest. "They just opened up a few months ago, and they cater to non-humans, so you wouldn't have to worry about trying to fit in and be human. You could be a little more of yourself without stressing out."

Well, there was some appeal in that. Lyla didn't have a lot of experience with trying to blend in. All her experience had been with work, which required her to be in full angel mode, not hiding. Not having to figure out just how to hide who she was would be a great advantage for her, and she would probably be able to better relax. Taking a moment, she flipped through the brochure, looking at the amenities the place had to offer. It really did seem nice, and if she was being forced to get away, this would certainly be a good place to start.

Looking back up, she saw Zimarra's impatient and excited face staring at her, waiting for her response. Lyla knew her friend had been waiting for the day the two of them could go off together and have fun. Why had she put it off for so long? "I have nothing to wear."

As if those words were some sort of secret signal of agreement, Zimarra jumped into the air, her wings flashing out in a flurry of bright glittering light as she danced in a circle before landing. "Leave it to me. We will get you all set up. Oh, I have to make a reservation for us too. Trust me, this is going to be amazing!"

Chapter 2

Lyla

Their angelic energy was still high with Christmas having not been too long ago and Easter just around the corner, and Lyla and Zimarra felt it in them when they arrived on Earth. It didn't usually start to wane some until closer to fall. They arrived a couple of days before their reservation at the resort to get Lyla plenty of clothes and other things they would need for their vacation. Now it was time for them to go to the resort, and Lyla felt her nervousness rising. Their reservations had them staying for a couple of weeks. After that, Zimarra wanted to take Lyla off to some other places around the world for the rest of their vacation.

The two of them ported onto the front walk of the resort. They were just outside of the main building where the resort's valet parking was set up. Huge stone walls had gorgeous waterfalls trickling down. The building was built from the redwoods, which surrounded the whole resort, helping it blend into the scenery. Accompanying the gorgeous wood were several large glass windows allowing in the bright sunlight. Lyla was in awe of just how beautiful it was. Sure, she had seen the pictures, but nothing compared to seeing it in person.

Stepping inside, she discovered the beauty continued inside the building. Lovely crystal chandeliers hung from the ceiling, and a massive four-sided fireplace, surrounded by chairs, was lit in the center. Lyla got so distracted by the opulence she didn't even realize Zimarra had dragged her over to the registration desk. A gorgeous woman, tall and blonde with a perfect body. stood behind the desk. Her clothes were high fashion and well put together, but it was the golden glow that surrounded her aura which gave away her angel status.

"Hello! Welcome to Crimson Moon Hideaway. We have your rooms set up already, so go on and get settled. Here is an itinerary for things we have going on during your stay. March is not a particularly busy month, considering the leprechauns have taken over, but we do have some wonderful live music going on in the Cave Bar tonight. I highly recommend checking that out," said the woman, whose name tag read Velvet. She slid a folder across the counter with a couple of sets of key cards placed on top.

Lyla picked up the folder, shifting the key card between two fingers as she opened the folder to look through the information. "Don't mind her. She hasn't spent a lot of personal time down here before," Zimarra said, but Lyla was too distracted to notice.

"Not to worry. One of the great things about this place is the fact you can be yourself. I'm sure both of you are going to have a great time, and maybe she will loosen up soon enough." Velvet's voice was filled with a warm and merry tone.

"That is my hope. Thank you for everything, and I think we might just check out that band tonight. Some music and dancing would do the both of us some good," Zimarra answered.

One of the bellmen came over and offered to help with their bags as well as show them to their rooms. Lyla was so out of it she aimlessly followed Zimarra and the bellman across the main lobby toward a set of elevators. "This particular set of elevators will bring you closer to your rooms," the bellman explained.

When they passed the main floor coffee shop, she swore she felt someone watching her. Looking up, she gazed around, trying to figure out who it could be, but she saw nothing out of the ordinary. Shrugging it off, she got on the elevator and rode up to their rooms. Lyla wasn't entirely sure why Zimarra had decided the two of them should have separate rooms, but she guessed it might be good to have some time to themselves. After all, as much as she loved her friend, she could be a bit much to handle.

"All right, get settled in, and we can meet up in a bit to explore before dinner tonight. I'm so excited we're doing this together!" Once again, Zimarra hugged her as if she could not get enough of her. It made Lyla happy her friend cared so much, but she also worried she would not be the best company.

Stepping into her room, she felt lost as to what to do next. An almost itching feeling pulled at her to check on her charges. A couple of her children lived a few hours south of where they were at, and she could sense them in her soul. It pained her deeply to not be working, but she didn't feel any sort of danger or need from any of her charges.

With a deep sigh, Lyla went about putting her clothes away in the dresser and closet, setting out her things, and making herself at home in her new temporary room. It was a lovely space overlooking a gorgeous pool area. Part of her felt a flutter of excitement, and a smile curved her lips. Maybe she could have a good time with this after all.

She had just finished getting her things put away when there was a soft knock on her door. Opening it up, she saw Zimarra dressed in her swimsuit with a towel draped over her arm.

"Isn't' it still a little cold for a swim?" Lyla arched a brow at her friend. While spring was starting to make itself known, the temperatures were still staying in the sixties.

"Pish, it isn't like we actually get cold; besides, there is a huge hot tub. I figured we could go relax some, have some drinks, and get a feel for the people here. I don't know about you, but I'm looking forward to finding someone to dance with tonight." Zimarra winked at her, and Lyla wasn't sure what the gesture was supposed to mean.

Instead of dwelling on it, she went back into her room, leaving the door open so Zimarra could follow, and pulled out her new swimsuit. Unlike Zimarra, who sported a revealing reddish-orange bikini that fit her coloring very well, Lyla had chosen something a little more modest. Her emerald-green one-piece covered her well and had a pretty design of white wave patterns on it. Like so much in her life, it was simple but worked for her.

"I still can't believe you wouldn't let me talk you into something a little more...exciting."

Lyla could feel the heat of her blush rising on her body and knew her skin had to be turning pink to match. No, they were not told to live some sort of celibate lifestyle away from the touch of another. However, Lyla had never experienced such things. While she knew Zimarra had, she had often changed the subject or simply avoided any conversation that would lead her friend to discussing her escapades of physical companionship. Part of the reason for this trip, at least for Zimarra, was to get Lyla to loosen up. At least, that was the impression she had gotten from her friend, but Lyla wasn't sure she was comfortable with that. It wasn't like she could bring whomever she spent time with on Earth back with her to Heaven.

"I'm happy with the suit I chose, and I think I look very pretty in it." Lyla wasn't about to say she felt safe in it. She knew a statement like that would only draw attention to the fact she was not comfortable with the idea of other people staring at her. Everyone could stare at Zimarra and stay away from her. It would make this whole forced vacation go a whole lot better.

"You always look pretty. That has never been the issue. The issue is, you very seldom try to look approachable or desirable. I know you're afraid, but there is nothing wrong with wanting to find love. You might actually find the experience worthwhile. I know I did."

The words shocked Lyla, and she found herself stopping short as she tried to finish her braid. Lyla knew Zimarra had partaken of physical relationships, but love? That had not been something her friend had ever shared with her before, and Lyla couldn't help but wonder if that was partly because she had pushed her away. As much as they were great friends in the matters of Heaven, Lyla had never been much of a friend when it came to Zimarra's Earthen escapades, and she was starting to see it had cost her a lot in the terms of their relationship. "I never knew you were in love."

"It was a long time ago, and I never told you about it because you have always been a bit sheepish when it came down to things here on Earth. But love is a beauty that we are blessed to get the opportunity to experience. You can keep yourself guarded through this whole trip and not experience anything, or you can try to live a little and maybe get your chance and experience the greatest gift of all. It is up to you. I, for one, am not going to waste my time here." Zimarra grabbed another towel and tossed it over to Lyla.

For a moment, Lyla thought she saw another emotion deep down in her friend's eyes. As much as her friend spoke about love with excitement, it seemed like part of it hurt. There was just so much behind her friend's words, and Lyla knew it. Not that it made it any easier for her to deal with. She had her own path to follow, and that didn't include getting involved with some stranger at a resort on Earth. Taking the towel Zimarra had tossed at her, she followed her friend down to the pool area. It was gorgeous, just like everything else. It looked like an oasis among all the trees. They walked past seating with heaters to keep the area warm. They continued toward the pool that gave way to a lazy river surrounding a much larger pool. To the left was a mountain structure covered in decorations and a waterfall, in the center sat a bar, and off to the right was the hot tub.

After grabbing a drink from the bar, the two of them made their way over to the hot tub and stepped into the steaming water. Lyla couldn't shake the strange feeling someone was watching her. Once again, she looked around, hoping to figure out who it was, but all she found were people going about their business. She was just about to give up when she saw them. Eyes filled with the flames of Hell.

Chapter 3

Ashford

"O ne black eye for Ashford!" the barista called out, catching his attention from where he had been scrolling his phone. Why he was suddenly obsessed with the stupid thing was beyond him, but it had become his normal morning routine. The dripped coffee with three shots of espresso, a bagel with cream cheese, and an hour or so of social media and news scrolling seemed to be a daily thing now. Not that there was really anything worth his time. He had seen the real shit stains the world had to offer and knew which ones were on their way to join the mix when their time came.

Getting up from his seat, he shoved his phone in his pocket and sauntered over to collect his coffee from the cute little human girl who worked behind the counter. She always seemed so shy, and that encouraged him to tease her. "Reading anything good today, Penny?" Ashford asked, lingering a little long when taking hold of his cup.

Penny smiled, her green eyes lighting up at the idea of talking about books. He had noticed on more than one occasion that, while she enjoyed her solitude, she often spent her time lost in another world reading a book. "No, still working through the same one from yesterday. It was getting good though before I had to put it down and come to work."

"Shame work seems to always get in the way of things," Ashford answered, a devilish smile crossing his lips, making the girl blush a bit. Yes, that always made his morning a bit better. "Well, thank you for breakfast once more. I'm sure I will see you again tomorrow."

He had just turned to head back to his seat when he heard Connak, one of the other baristas. Usually, the idle chatter and gossip wouldn't have drawn his attention, but something about his words piqued Ashford's curiosity. "Now, that isn't something you see every day. Guardian angels. Wow. And aren't they beautiful."

It wasn't at all odd to see angels on Earth. There was even one who worked the front desk of the resort. However, guardian angels were not known for leaving their post much. Many were said to be married to their work. In all his time since the fall, Ashford had never seen a guardian angel, which said a lot. While he had spent a large portion of his time in Hell, doing the bidding of his master, he had also spent a fair share of time on Earth, causing mischief and living life. After all, how better to learn to torture than to first understand who and what you were torturing?

With his curiosity now on high alert, Ashford walked toward the fireplace in the center of the room so he could get a better look. One of the angels, the one with the darker features, seemed calm and collected as she handled all the paperwork while pulling her friend along. Maybe she had been to Earth before. The other, well, she seemed in awe. She looked around her as if seeing the world for the first time. The expression of pure amazement was so innocent and cute that it was nearly sickening. How could anyone —even an angel—be that pure?

Taking a drink from his coffee, he couldn't take his eyes off the blonde. She was a beautiful thing and very much a contrast to him. His skin was a darker tan, and his nearly black hair had the faintest hint of copper highlights that shone only in certain light. Then there were his eyes. While hers looked like pools of the sky, his were of flame, orange, blue, and purple, dancing and giving away the dangerous creature he was. He was very much amused by how mystified the little angel seemed to be. A chuckle rose in him, and he took a seat so he could enjoy the show. That could certainly make things fun. It had been a very long time since he got to truly corrupt someone. Maybe he could pull it off. Or, feeling a tinge of reservation, he could stay the course as to why he had left Hell to begin with.

While he ran his fingers through his thick dark hair, his mind wandered back to a few weeks ago. It wasn't like his boredom with Hell was a sudden and new change in him. He had dealt with boredom before. After some time and a break, things always evened back out. This time was different. Things had changed, and he could not go back. Not that Hell made a habit of handing out retirement packages and tickets to Florida. Ashford was very aware of the target his decision put on his back. It was part of what drew him to Crimson Moon Hideaway. Something about the place made him feel safe and like he could lay low for a while.

That and it was close to the people he needed to be nearby.

The angels had finished their business at the front desk and were making their way toward the elevators. Not wanting to come off like a stalker, he kept his head down, as if he were looking at his coffee cup instead of them. It didn't keep him from watching her graceful movement as she walked, still with a look of childlike wonder on her face. Something about the whole scene made him tingle, but he wasn't sure what that was. Ashford waited until the door to the elevator closed before making his way over to watch the numbers change as the elevator lifted to different floors. Interesting, they were on the same floor he was.

Pressing the button so he could go back to his room as well, he couldn't help but be curious whether they were close to each other on the floor. He had heard rumors of people "happening" to find love when visiting this place. Not that he felt worthy of anything of the sort. No, he was nothing but filth and degradation, meant to spend the rest of what little life he had left alone and unwanted.

Shrugging it off, he rode the elevator up to his floor and went to his room, feeling sorrier for himself than he cared to admit. His coffee now held a rancid taste in his mouth, and he poured it down the sink. He stormed around the room, uncertain as to where the foul mood had really come from. One thing was certain, he had made his choices, and he now knew he had to live with them.

He flopped down on the bed and took in a deep breath, taking in the scent of all the redwoods that made up and surrounded this place. Once, twice, three times, and he finally started to feel a calm come over him. There was magic here, powerful magic, and it had brought him an overwhelming sense of peace. At least until that little angel showed up. Now his mind didn't want to shut down.

He continued his slow, calculated breathing, attempting to push back the frustration, until he heard them. The sound of their melodious voices giggling about heading down to the hot tub made something burn deep inside of him. Damn, he wasn't sure he had ever felt a desire this strong, and it was starting to make him extremely angry.

Getting up, he decided if she was going to distract him, then, by Hell, he was going to distract her.

He changed into his swim trunks quickly and grabbed a towel before marching down to the pool area. It was still a bit early in the day for drinks, so that would have to wait until later. Once he stepped out near the hot tub and got a full view of the angel in her simple one-piece swimsuit, his head spun. What was happening to him? He could almost feel the fire burning in his eyes, and he knew the moment she saw him because the shocked look on her face gave it away. Apparently, she saw the flames as well.

Strutting over to the two of them, he let a grin cross his face a moment before he began to step into the hot tub. "I hope you don't mind if I join you. I'm feeling a bit stiff and want to loosen up before tonight."

Ashford watched as the blonde attempted to find her words, but her friend had no problems. "Not at all, there is certainly plenty of room. I'm Zimarra. This is Lyla. We just got here today."

He was positive they knew what he was, so it surprised him at how pleasant she was being with him. "Well, I got here just after Valentine's Day, and I certainly can say it has been wonderful."

"Oh, an extended stay. Why is that?" Zimarra asked, seeming genuinely curious.

"Sometimes you just need a break from it all. I certainly could use some time away. What about you two?" Though the woman with the darker hair was talking, he couldn't help but glance over to the other one. He had to bite his tongue to keep from laughing when her friend nudged her with her elbow.

"Oh, um, I was ordered to take a vacation, so here we are. Zimarra had heard about this place and thought it would be nice. So far, it is though we have only been here a couple of hours," Lyla said, her voice almost a whisper. If not for his ability to hear so well, he probably wouldn't have heard her.

"She's a bit shy. Give her time. The girl has never taken a vacation," Zimarra added with a hint of laughter in her voice.

"Well, I'm sure it won't take long before she starts to feel more relaxed. Sometimes it just takes a while to get acclimated. Maybe come out tonight? There is supposed to be some music and dancing." Ashford turned and smiled at Lyla. His eyes lingered intensely on her. He wasn't sure what it was, but something about their exchange had Lyla blushing. Well, it was possible she was just overheated from the hot tub, but he was pretty certain the conversation had turned her skin that lovely shade of pink. Either way, the color on her cheeks made her look even more beautiful than she had before, which was both exciting and frustrating.

"Oh yes, we talked about possibly going there tonight." The blonde angel bit her lip, making it swell some and look much more enticing. "Maybe we will see you there?"

It seemed nervousness got the best of her, as she quickly got out of the hot tub. Her friend laughed before joining her, and the two of them got their towels. As much as he hated to see the girl go, he had to admit he enjoyed the view. Damn, she was one sexy angel. Were you even allowed to call angel's sexy? Not that he cared. Ashford didn't make a habit out of following the rules.

Now that he had plans for the night, Ashford needed to get a nap. His blood was rushing through his body, and he had every intention of getting in a few dances with that angel. Maybe he would even sneak a kiss if the right moment presented itself. Fuck! What in all of Hell had come over him? The resort was really starting to get to him.

"I have just never had anyone look at me that way or talk to me that way for that matter. It was strange and uncomfortable." Lyla sighed.

"Well, that is because you have no experience with anything. Lyla, I hate to say it, but you haven't been here for any other reason than work. You have no idea what it is like to feel and experience something more than yourself," Zimarra said, almost scaring Lyla.

"But he is a demon." Lyla wasn't sure what else to say.

"I'm not saying run off and fall for the guy. I'm saying dance with him and enjoy something other than work for a change. That is all. Jeez, this isn't supposed to be a punishment."

Lyla didn't really know what else to say, so she didn't say anything at all. Realizing she was done with the conversation, Zimarra moved things along. They still needed to get changed for dinner later and then for some time out. Lyla thought she might get a bit of rest before their evening activities, seeing they had been going nonstop all day. After Zimarra left the room, Lyla curled up in a chair to overlook the beauty of the resort and rest. Her mind raced, constantly thinking about that demon and the strange sensations he had made her feel.

***

Lyla had never worn anything quite like the

dress she had picked out for dinner and dancing tonight. She looked in the mirror and took a moment to smooth her hands over the long white dress that hugged her curves. There was an inlay of gold and silver, which made it shine even in the dimmest light. She felt fancy and sophisticated. It was certainly a far cry from her usual plain look. With one last touch-up to the glitter she had placed on her eyelids, she left her room and caught Zimarra heading in her direction.

"Well now, don't you look nice," Zimarra said, giving Lyla a friendly hug as they met up in the hall.

"I certainly feel different," Lyla answered, feeling her cheeks warm. "You look incredible as well, but you always do."

Zimarra had chosen to wear a black dress with a blue flame pattern in sequins over the bottom part. It was stunning, and Lyla couldn't help but admire it.

The two of them walked together to the elevator, and as they made their way down to the main floor, Lyla's heart raced more and more. It wasn't just the adrenaline for the dancing later in the night. No, she also felt anxiety about seeing the demon again. All afternoon, his face had invaded her thoughts. No one had ever impacted her so strongly before, and it was highly unnerving. However, that didn't mean she wanted to run into him again. Staying away from him was probably all for the best.

The elevator bell rang, making her jump a bit, before the doors opened, and they were greeted with a rush of people. There were certainly far more people out and about now that evening had fallen. Guests were coming to and fro, heading for the restaurants and out to the pool. Everything was far livelier than it had been earlier. Lyla even had to skip out of the way of a small man holding what she swore was a pot of gold as he rushed toward where the conference rooms were.

Finally, they were seated for dinner at Skippers Restaurant, the higher end of the two restaurants in the resort. They had just ordered their drinks when Lyla looked up and saw him. Ashford was standing at the entrance to the restaurant, speaking with a beautiful dark-skinned woman. Zimarra leaned over so she could whisper to Lyla, but it took her a moment to register what her friend said. "That is Jianna, the owner. I have heard she is a bit of a matchmaker."

There was a teasing tone in her friend's voice, which had Lyla rolling her eyes. That was until the woman walked Ashford toward their table, seating him at the table next to theirs. He was dressed in a well-fitting pair of black slacks with a dark button-up shirt. It was spun with hints of red, orange, and blue, something she guessed was meant to match his eyes. The moment he took his seat, he looked over to them and motioned as if to ask to join them. Lyla was about to say no, but Zimarra quickly answered for him to come over.

"No one should be alone at dinner. Come have a seat with us.

"Well, the both of you look beautiful tonight. I have to say I feel lucky to be seated at the table with the two of you," Ashford said, reaching out and taking a sip of the complimentary water that had been placed on the tables. He had chosen the chair closest to Lyla's, and the heat of him so near had her body tensing.

Lyla blushed, and Zimarra giggled quietly and nudged her with her toe under the table. Ignoring her friend's teasing, she turned to their new table mate. "Thank you. You look very nice as well."

The waiter brought their drinks, temporarily interrupting their conversation, and then they ordered dinner. "Well, I'm glad you like my outfit. I have to say I have been getting a lot of compliments tonight. The owner even mentioned that I seemed to have a spring in my step. Maybe I was just excited to have someone to meet up with tonight."

"I get the feeling you always look good like this, but it is nice that you are feeling good as well. I'm a bit nervous about tonight. I'm not sure I have ever really gone dancing before." Lyla tried her best to hold a conversation while her stomach did somersaults inside of her.

"There really isn't anything to it. I'm sure you will be more than fine. My name is Ashford, by the way. I don't think I ever really got around to mentioning that earlier," the demon said, reaching his hand out to shake hers.

"Oh, I'm Lyla, and that is Zimarra." She felt silly having not realized such a basic thing. When she remembered Zimarra had already told him their names, she blushed again, but they were thankfully interrupted by the waiter bringing out their meals.

Lyla's mouth watered at the smell of the food as it was placed before her. As she breathed the aroma in, a smile spread over her lips before she picked up her fork and began to eat. She moaned as she took the first bite and then blushed deeper when she saw the look Ashford was giving her. It was apparent he was amused by her.

About halfway through his meal, Ashford pushed his food away and took another drink. The look in Ashford's eyes had butterflies fluttering in Lyla's stomach, and she pushed her food away as well.

"I think we should go dance." Ashford smacked his hands down on the table before standing and holding his hand out to her.

Lyla stared up at him, wide-eyed and cautious. He was a demon. There was no way she could dance with him. Zimarra nearly pushed her out of her chair. "Go! Have fun. I'll take care of the check then meet the two of you over there."

The wicked look on Ashford's face at her friend's words went right to her core, but she ignored it and reached out, taking Ashford's hand and standing. "Sure, um, let's dance."

There was energy between them as he guided

her out of the restaurant and toward the Cave Bar. The bar had been appropriately named, looking much larger than it had appeared on the little map they had been given. Lyla instantly felt like they had entered a cave with the walls lined with stone. Blue lights accented everything including large slabs of flowing water that sat on either side of the bar. The dance floor was made of glass and lit with blue light, all of which had her glowing as if her power was riding her.

Twirling her around until they were faced toward each other, Ashford took a moment to soak in how she looked. The look on his face was a little unsettling at first, as if he was ready to eat her. Then his features smoothed and became more relaxed. His arm encircled her waist, pulling her close, and for some reason she couldn't put her finger on, she felt safe. It made no sense at all, but with him holding her, she didn't want to question it. Ashford surprised her by also being a gentleman and keeping one hand on her waist while he held her hand with the other.

"Do I make you nervous?" Ashford asked, stepping in a little closer to her as he whispered close to her ear.

"I'm not sure." She was sure she was going to end up burning someone if she continued to blush the way she was.

"Don't be. This is just a party. I'm sure I can't do too much damage in one night." He chuckled a bit as he responded. "Well, that is, unless you want me to."

"Um, no, that is okay. I don't think that would be a good idea." She stumbled, and he reached out to hold her steady.

"Don't fall. I was only having a little fun with you. Lighten up. This is supposed to be a vacation, is it not?" His words were whispered so close to her face she could feel his breath on her lips. A burning, tingling sensation raced down to the pit of her soul.

They got lost dancing again. Everything around them seemed to disappear, time slipped away, and she couldn't stop the smile that spread over her face. Ashford was handsome, graceful, and charming in ways she hadn't expected. Part of her knew she should be careful; he was a demon and demons wanted nothing more than to pull others down with them, but it didn't feel that way.

No, it felt like part of him hoped to rise with her.

The sound of people cheering broke through the haze they were in. At first, she wasn't sure what they were screaming for. The fast music ended, and a slower song started. A wicked smile spread over his face, and the crowd calmed. Lyla's breath caught when Ashford's lips pressed to hers and his body became flush to hers. At first, she jumped, surprised by the action, but he kept her in his arms and slowly deepened the kiss. Lyla had never been kissed before, but he guided her, and she became lost in it.

It was magical and beautiful, and it was interrupted all too quickly when he pulled away, reaching behind him, and cried out in pain. She wasn't sure what had happened until he pulled his hand in front of him and she saw blood on it. He dropped to one knee and toppled over.

Chapter 5

Ashford

Lyla tasted like the Heaven he had given up all those millennia ago. All he wanted, all he could think about, was being with her. Even his desire to fall had not been as strong as the desire he felt now. It had him dropping his guard, and therein lay his mistake. The joyous momentum of their night had him lost in the feel of kissing her and holding her. He never wanted it to stop, but a sting of white-hot pain sliced through his back, and the faintest words were whispered in his ear. "We are coming for you. Come home, or the next attack will be worse."

His attacker was gone as quickly as they had come, and Ashford pulled away from Lyla as he reached behind him. When he took his hand from his back, it came away soaked in blood. The blade had struck true and deep. If he had been human, it would have been a killing blow, but he wasn't human. Didn't mean it wasn't going to hurt like a son of a bitch while he healed from it. Demon blades were one of the few things that could put a demon down.

He wasn't sure how he managed to hold himself up as long as he did, but he saw the look of fear and shock on Lyla's face a moment before his knees buckled and he went down. The people around them seemed to be none the wiser, focused on their own romances, but Lyla had eyes only for him. She knelt next to him, her hand on his chest for support, and looked behind him to check out the wound. "Ashford, what happened?"

"Ah, just got too bloody excited," he groaned, but his body shook in pain.

"You need help. Just hang on," Lyla said. The beautiful blue light that always seemed to hum from her aura illuminated brighter even through all of the lights in the bar. Her warm hand pressed tighter against his chest a moment before the light painfully engulfed him, and then he was lying on a bed, facedown. From the looks of it, though, it wasn't his bed. Of course, she didn't know which room was his.

"Don't think me forward, but I need to get a better look at this." Lyla didn't give him much time to answer before she pulled his shirt up. It was tight, and she was forced to use magic to remove the clothing the rest of the way.

"I see you just want to get me out of my clothes." Ashford tried to chuckle but hissed as pain coursed through him.

"This is a pretty deep wound, and I'm not able to heal it. Maybe I can sew you up though. I think I have a sewing kit in the bathroom." Lyla ignored his somewhat flirtatious remark.

"I don't do my own tailoring, so I don't think I will be of any use." Ashford groaned, pulling a pillow to him so he could rest his head better.

"Give me a moment." He felt the moment she walked away from him as the room grew cold. He turned his head to watch her as she made her way to the bathroom. Damn, she had no idea just how sexy she was. Here she was, all business, and all he could think about was how much he wanted to get his hands on her again.

A few moments later, she came back with a small sewing case and some washcloths. He watched her as she took a seat next to him and pulled out a needle. Light enveloped the needle, and it bent like a fishhook. He had to look away as the sensation of purity sizzled over him. It ached of memories long gone, but he didn't want her to see that in his eyes. "So, you are going to stitch me up?"

"I'm going to try to. Do you have any idea why this happened?" Lyla asked, threading the needle. She took time to clean the wound before going any further, and he hissed at the pressure of her hand on it.

"I'm a demon. I can name a million people and reasons for this to happen." She wouldn't understand the truth. He had left Hell and had no intentions of going back. Of course, there were other secrets he wasn't ready to share with others either.

A soft look covered Lyla's face as she began to gingerly stitch up the wound. "That may be true, but I have a feeling this may be a bit more specific."

"One might think you actually care about the fact I was hurt." Ashford hissed as the needle slid in and out of his skin.

"I do care. I don't like to see anyone get hurt," Lyla answered, steadily sticking to her work. She was good, cautious, and he knew without a doubt the stitches would heal leaving very little of a scar.

Part of him wanted to be bitter at her answer; he believed she would say the same thing to anyone, but maybe she wouldn't. Maybe part of her actually cared. He bit back the snarky words threatening to leak from between his lips. They stayed in a comfortable silence for several moments as Lyla continued to work on him. Distantly, the sounds of the resort still bustling with people could be heard, and he wished he was still on the dance floor with her. That was all he had thought about all day, and closing his eyes, he did his best to picture a much better night.

The pain was starting to subside, so he could relax some. Taking a shallow breath so not to disturb her stitching, he broke the silence. "So, I see how it is. One kiss, and you couldn't wait to get me in your bed."

A gasp escaped her, and he hissed as she

accidentally stuck him with the needle. Ashford could almost feel the blush rise on her, and he excused her misstep with the sewing for his amusement at making her feel a bit uncomfortable. "I just wasn't sure where to take you. I didn't know where your room was, and you needed help."

"Oh, so you wanted to go back to my room? We could do that." He continued to tease her and laughed when she let out a huff of frustration.

"How am I supposed to take care of you when you are being so...so..."

"So what?" He turned so he could look up at her through his hair, a wicked grin on his face. "Charming. Sexy. Desirable."

"Incorrigible."

"Well, there is that, but I like to think that what I said is more accurate." Ashford chuckled.

Finally, Lyla finished, and she once again retreated to the bathroom. Getting up gingerly, he stood on shaky legs before he went to check out the stitches in the mirror. Turning, he saw the length of the wound. Not too bad, considering how much it hurt. There was blood staining down from it and below his pants line, but it was nothing a shower wouldn't take care of. Lyla came back out, holding a wet cloth, and came over to him. "Here, let me clean you up some at least. I'm sure that doesn't feel very good."

"You don't have to do all that. As it is, you have already gone out of your way to patch me up." He didn't stop her when she started to run the warm wet cloth over him. More heat rose in him, heat that made his eyes blaze.

"I already told you. I want to help. Besides, I need to make sure it looks good and isn't going to pop open after you leave," Lyla answered, but her words were breathy, making him turn to face her again.

He licked his lips, and without thinking, he moved in and began to kiss her again. This time, he hoped the kiss could last. He wrapped his arms around her, pulling her tight as he deepened the kiss, tasting her and craving more. Part of him wanted to push for more, but he knew his luck was not that good. Instead, he kissed her until the two of them were thoroughly lost in it. Then, with great pains, he pulled away. "I should go."

Lyla nodded as if trying to gain her sanity. He didn't try to make her answer him. Instead, he gave her one more kiss then walked to the door. With one last smile, he exited the room. Damn, the girl was in the room right next to his. What the fuck was going on here? Was it more than just luck? He wasn't sure, but he certainly wasn't ready to put any more stock into it.

Just as Ashford closed the door to his room, he saw Lyla's friend coming down the hall. He had good timing getting out of there, even if all he could think about was how badly he wanted to get back into her room.

Chapter 6

Lyla

L yla's fingers rubbed over where Ashford had just kissed her. She was so stunned it barely registered he had left. It wasn't until the room felt empty that she realized he had left. Taking a couple of deep breaths, she tried to get her head back on straight, when someone knocked on her door, she jumped. Heart pounding, she raced to answer it, but a tinge of disappointment hit when she saw it was only Zimarra.

"Well, nice to see you too. Are you okay?"

She wasn't sure. She was physically okay, but emotionally, that was something completely different. Whatever had happened between her and Ashford, it certainly had stirred something inside of her that had laid dormant most of her life. "I think so. I just. Well. I was dancing with Ashford, and then someone stabbed him. I didn't see who it was."

"Of course, you didn't. You were kissing him. Don't think I didn't see what was happening." The playful tone in her friend's voice did not make it any less embarrassing.

"Um, well, it sort of just happened. And didn't you say I should just loosen up?" Of course, Zimarra probably hadn't meant for her to start making out with the demon. Dancing was one thing, but kissing was something else.

"Yeah, but not a kiss like that." Zimarra continued to tease her, but Lyla swore she also heard concern in her friend's voice.

Deciding not to continue to let her shyness and embarrassment get to her, she decided to just laugh. "Well, whatever it was, Ashford got hurt, so I brought him up here and stitched him up."

"You brought him up to your room? Well then. You do realize there is something between the two of you. I can feel it, and I'm just an innocent bystander." Zimarra sat in one of the chairs by the window. "I know it bothers you, but I think ignoring it will bother you more."

"We aren't allowed to pursue such things, and with a demon, nonetheless. This is a vacation, and yes, I enjoyed some of tonight. It doesn't mean anything." Even as she said it, pain stabbed through her. There was no way her life would ever be the same now that she had found Ashford. Something about losing him tore her apart.

"Nothing says we can't do anything. We have a job, and so long as we do what is asked of us, we don't have to be automatons with no life. You chose that. You have holed yourself up in Heaven doing nothing but work for a millennium. Maybe there is a reason you were sent on leave right now. Have you ever thought of that?" Zimarra was a big believer in there being more to things than face value. They had often spoken about it, but Lyla wasn't sure she felt the same way.

Even if she was meant to come down here and find someone, it certainly shouldn't have been a demon. Nothing about that made any sense to her. Or maybe Zimarra was right after all. Maybe she had been brought here because Ashford needed her. Why had he been attacked? What was he hiding? Ashford had made a point to not really answer any of her questions. She believed he was trying to keep something important from her. Now even more confused, she sat next to her friend and rested her head on her shoulder.

"Lyla, I love you, but at some point, you have to see there is more out there. I hate seeing you alone."

"I don't know how to not be alone," Lyla whispered with a deep sigh, and her eyes closed. It was getting late, and she needed sleep. She needed to not worry so much, but part of her was afraid whoever had come to hurt Ashford would come back to finish the job. She should have walked him to his room. Then at least she would be able to check in on him. Of course, she could sense him out, but that was considered a bit rude.

"Hey, why don't you get some sleep. It has been a long night. Maybe some rest will help you put some things in perspective?" Zimarra kissed the top of her head and then left to go to her room.

Of course, she was right. Lyla needed sleep. They had gotten up early and been going strong all day. Her friend hadn't been gone long before Lyla was in bed, eyes closed and ready to sleep. As she drifted off to sleep, all she could think about were those sensual kisses with the forbidden demon.

✳✳✳

Ashford

Ashford sat looking out of the window, his mind wandering through the day. When he had woken up, he had thought it would be another normal day for him—food, fun, and ending the night with some music and dancing. He certainly hadn't expected to find Lyla. Nor had he planned on getting stabbed in the back, but he should have expected an attack. They had left him alone for a while, and it was about time someone came looking for him. His boredom with his life back in Hell and the way he had left didn't hide the fact he wasn't planning to come back.

That meant he had signed his own death warrant, but anything was better than an eternity torturing the same sorts of lowlifes, over and over, doing the bidding of mid-level demon lords on power trips. It was time for him to be his own man, even if it was only for a short time. That was exactly what he had been doing since he had left. No matter how short his time was, it would have to be lived his way.

Pulling his phone out, he flipped through some pictures he had taken a little less than a year ago. The small infants in the pictures were another part of the reason for his exodus from Hell. They had been the product of a crazy night. Honestly, it had been a mistake but one he would never regret. Even if he had only gotten to see his children the one time.

Staying away from them was meant to keep them safe. If no one knew about them, then no one would go after them. Smiling down at the photo, he went to bed, knowing he had worn out the day. He had just started to fall asleep when he felt the energy enter his room.

"Well now. You certainly are getting a little on the careless side. Honestly, Ashford, I would have thought you would be more cautious than this," a sensual female voice said, waking him from his near sleep.

Having been so close to sleep, it was difficult for him to pull himself out of the state. When he finally managed to get his eyes open, he saw her looking through his phone. "What are you doing here, Cassandra?"

The demon was gorgeous with long legs, creamy skin, long blood-red hair, and deep-green cat eyes. A wicked smile spread over her lips. "I wanted to see how close to death you were after our meeting earlier tonight."

"I'm not dead. Now what are you doing here? I'm not going back." Ashford groaned, sitting up some.

"Maybe, or maybe you will find stronger motivation. As I said, Ashford, you aren't being very cautious." Cassandra chuckled wickedly before tossing the phone on the bed next to him.

Grabbing the phone, he saw it was on the picture of his children. He looked up to protest, but she was gone just as quickly as she had come. No, this was not going to happen. They could do whatever they wanted to him, but there was no way he would let anything happen to his children.

Chapter 7

Lyla

L yla woke with a start; her heart raced and her blue light flared, illuminating the room. It only happened when one of her charges was in danger, and every nerve in her body was on fire. Of course, she wasn't supposed to be working. The orders had been to take time off, but how could she ignore a threat to one of her charges? Everything in her was screaming for her to go see about them.

Despite her orders, she was going to check. Closing her eyes, she tried to pinpoint where the signal was coming from. It wasn't far, just down in San Francisco. Surely, she could check on things and be back before anyone really noticed she was gone. After all, it was still early, and most everyone had been up extremely late due to the party. Walking over to her closet, she went through her clothes and got dressed in her usual guardian clothes of white pants and a longer coat-style white shirt with a light-blue belt. To finish off the look, she pulled her hair up in a high ponytail.

Once dressed, she took a deep breath and teleported out to the home of her charges. She landed in the backyard near the air-conditioning unit and where they kept the garbage can. It was a smaller backyard, which was common in this area. The houses were close together, and the street was typically busy. The children had an upstairs bedroom, so she would have to go up there to see what was going on, but she wanted to check out the area first. Nothing out of the ordinary was happening on the first floor, so she flew up to the bedroom window to peek inside. Then she saw him.

Ashford sat in a rocking chair in the corner of the room, watching the children with a serious look on his face. The dark circles under his eyes were evidence of the fact he hadn't slept. However, she was more concerned with why he was in their bedroom eyeing her charges. The two children, a sweet set of twins with dark hair and eyes, were sleeping peacefully in their beds. Lyla had been watching over them since their birth and had grown very fond of them.

Ashford's head dropped for a second before he jerked it up, his eyes blinking. His exhaustion threatened to win. Needing answers, Lyla teleported into the room next to him and knelt. "What are you doing here?"

The demon jumped, obviously caught off guard by her being there. "I could ask you the same question. Shouldn't you be enjoying your vacation?"

"These are two of my charges, and I felt they were threatened. I'm here to protect them. So again. Why are you here?" Lyla asked, her voice holding a tinge of her power. No matter the strange feelings she had for the demon, her charges came first.

"They are my children. I am watching them because the people who attacked me last night threatened them. I have been here since I left you."

It hadn't been the answer she expected, and she turned to look at him. Of course, she had heard of demons having children before, but most of the time, they took them off to Hell with them. These children had been left on Earth to live normal lives. Why had he done that?

"What do you mean they're your children?" Lyla asked, still a bit shocked by his answer.

"I mean just that. They are my children. I had a bit of a fling with their mother the last time I took a break from Hell, and they were the product of that. While I don't share true feelings for their mother, I do very much care for them. They are part of the reason I chose to leave Hell and why I am now being hunted."

It was all starting to make sense to her. He had been attacked because he was trying to leave his position in Hell. They wanted to take him down since he was breaking his contract. Demons were bound by their contracts, and following through with their duty in Hell was required. Angels, in a way, were the same. They were devoted to God, but it was a point of honor for them. For demons, it seemed to be more like a prison they had been pulled into with lies and promises of freedom. At least, that was Lyla's perception of it. For all she knew, she could be completely wrong on that.

"So, they aren't happy that you want to leave Hell and be here with your children?" Lyla asked, trying to make sure she understood the situation.

"They aren't happy I want to leave Hell because I am no longer happy there. I used to love my life there, but, well, not anymore, not for a very long time. Hurting and corrupting people used to be fun; I never lost a wink of sleep. Now something changed. I'm having nightmares and find myself having guilty thoughts. It is time for a change, and I am just ready for something different. I don't want to be there anymore, and they don't seem to understand or care about that." Ashford leaned back in the chair and closed his eyes. "What are the odds that you would be my children's guardian angel? Everything about life since meeting you has just been strange."

Lyla didn't know what to say to that, mostly because she agreed. Ashford made her feel things she shouldn't, but she desperately tried to ignore it. Sitting there with him, watching over his children, it was harder to push the feelings away, and hearing his reasons for wanting to leave Hell made her want to help him even more. "I have to agree. I have never had an experience like the one I had last night. Well, before the stabbing. Makes me wonder if God knew that I was meant to find you."

"I highly doubt God had anything to do with something involving me, but pretty to think so." There was a bitter tone in Ashford's voice, and it reminded her of his fallen status. Did part of him want to find a way to rise again, or had he really been that upset about life up in Heaven? Lyla had never really understood the reasons behind why some of the angels had chosen to fall. Sure, the temptation had sounded worthwhile, but nothing about it sounded worth giving up all they had. At least not to her.

Once again, Ashford started to nod off, and again, he forced himself awake. She watched as his grip on the chair tightened to what seemed a painful level. His knuckles turned white, and he stood up and twisted his body, popping his back. A speckle of blood showed through his white T-shirt. The stitches had popped, and maybe that had been on purpose. Obviously, he was trying to keep himself awake.

"You need sleep. There is no way you can protect them like this," Lyla whispered, standing next to him.

"Their mother will be awake soon. I need to speak with her and let her know what is going on. If I can get her to understand, maybe I can do more. So far, I haven't seen Cassandra, but that doesn't mean she isn't disguising herself in the shadows. She is rather powerful." Ashford stretched again, making more blood seep through his shirt.

"Who is Cassandra? Is that who attacked you?" Lyla asked.

"Yeah, she is a hunter demon. When a demon goes rogue, she is sent after them to either drag them back to Hell or kill them for good. Last night was a warning. She is going to keep making things bad for me until she either gets me to go back or realizes I'm not going to." There was a hit of sadness and finality in Ashford's voice. He wasn't afraid of what would happen to him, but he certainly wouldn't let anything happen to his children. It was something Lyla could get behind. Leaning into him, she gave him a gentle hug.

"Well, I am going to do the best I can to help take care of them." She kissed his cheek, not even sure why she did it. Then she heard noise coming from down the hall. It was clear Ashford had heard it too as he straightened up and got ready to confront whoever was coming. Lyla was fairly certain it would be the mother. Deciding it best to stay out of sight, she stepped back and faded so she would not be visible to the woman. A few moments later, the woman walked into the room, then stopped, and stared at Ashford.

Chapter 8

Ashford

"What are you doing here?" Becca asked from just inside the bedroom door. Ashford hadn't seen Becca since just after the kids had been born. She was a pretty woman, a little on the short side, with a few curves but nothing too large. Her hair was a mass of reddish-blonde curls and her eyes were a light brown.

Ashford shoved his hands in his pockets, looking a bit sheepish at having broken into the house when he shouldn't have been there in the first place. After the kids had been born and he confessed what he was, he had sworn to stay away. Becca didn't want him to influence them with his demon heritage. It was something he could easily understand, but it wasn't something he was happy to hear at the time. Now, his life was threatening to break into their world anyway. Becca deserved to know their children were in danger and how he intended to keep them safe.

"That isn't an answer, Ashford. You told me you were going to stay away." Becca crossed her arms over her chest.

"Something has happened, and I wanted to come and make sure the kids were okay," Ashford whispered, looking over at his kids still sleeping.

"Why wouldn't they be okay? What have you done?" Becca's accusing tone cut deep to his soul—if he really had a soul.

"I left. I could not take it anymore, and I left Hell, and there are certain people who are not happy about it. I am going to take care of it, but I think the kids need to be better protected." Ashford tried to explain. He knew Becca wouldn't fully understand, and he didn't expect her to. He just hoped she would realize he only wanted to protect them. Keep them safe. "If the people who are after me were to come here, you wouldn't be able to stop them. I really think..."

"Don't you dare. There is no way I am going to let you take them from me. They are my kids." Becca fought back, moving between him and the little ones.

"I'm not saying that. They are your kids, but they are my children too. I need to take them temporarily. They are special, and I want them safe. I also have the help of others who have the power to keep them safe in a way that you just can't. Please believe me. The last thing I want to do is take them away, but I would feel worse if something horrible happened and I didn't do everything I could to keep them safe." Ashford pleaded, moving in closer to her. "I know what happened between the two of us was fleeting, and we made some mistakes. However, despite what I am, I'm not heartless. I do care and love them."

He watched the anger bristle over the woman before him. There was no doubt Becca was struggling between her determination to be a strong powerful mother and her knowledge of the world her children really belonged to. It was a hard pill to swallow—one Ashford had hoped he wouldn't have had to shove down her throat for many years. Of course, he knew one day their powers would manifest, and then she would need help, but he was hoping that day would come later.

"The children will be safe, and once everything is taken care of, I will bring them back. Please. You know I wouldn't be here if it wasn't truly important."

"Where are you going to take them?" Becca asked, her resolve starting to falter.

"Honestly, I am going to take them to this vacation place I have been staying at. It is really beautiful and fun. I know the kids are still quite young, but I'm sure they will enjoy it. I will do all I can to make sure of it."

"So, your solution to them being in danger is to take them on a vacation. Doesn't sound like you are trying to keep them safe." Becca pushed him back a bit.

"Well, that is where I am staying right now,

and I have some friends there that are going to help me keep them safe." Ashford was starting to get annoyed especially since he was starting to repeat himself too much.

"Are these friends of yours like you?" Becca asked, tapping him on the chest.

"No, in fact. My friends couldn't be further away from me as far as power and personality." Ashford felt the fissure of energy first, and out of the corner of his eye, he saw Lyla approach. Her beautiful blue glow was nearly blinding in its ethereal essence.

The calm Lyla brought into the room was palpable. Even he could sense it, and part of him felt sick from it, but that was the dark part inside of him. The other part of him was elated she was there for him.

"Hello, Becca, you may not know who I am, but my name is Lyla. I have never revealed myself like this to a parent before, but I am the guardian angel for your children. I am going to help Ashford care for them while they are in danger. It is my duty."

Part of Becca wanted to protest, but Ashford could see that something about Lyla's purity spoke to Becca in a way nothing else could. It was magical. The shock on Becca's face made Ashford want to chuckle. "I...I can't believe this. I didn't think this was real." Becca shuddered and reached for Lyla.

"I understand what you are going through

must be terrifying. You want your children to be safe and with you. However, I want your children to always be safe. Can you please trust that I will do that for you?" Lyla took Becca's hand.

"You promise?" Becca asked, tears forming in her eyes.

"I do. We are going to do everything for them. You have nothing to worry about." The most beautiful smile he had ever seen spread over Lyla's face, making him want to pull her to him, but that would have been a little tactless and rude.

"Well, let me get some of their things together so they will have everything they need." Becca went to the closet and pulled out a couple of bags. She filled them with the various things the two small children would need.

Ashford watched in amazement. When they left, he would be on his own with his kids. Well, not completely. Lyla had offered to be there for him, but he had never taken care of his kids before. He had no idea what they did and didn't like. Nor did he know how to tell when they needed something. They were barely a year old; how was he supposed to know when they needed something?

Lyla placed her hand on his shoulder. It was a reassuring gesture, letting him know that, no matter how nervous he was, she would be there with him to make sure nothing went wrong. Of course, he knew they would also be fighting off the demons after him, but at least he knew where the kids would be and that they would be protected by others with enough power to take on his enemies. It was more than he could ask for and more than he deserved.

Lyla had come into his life at just the right time for him and his children. Ashford had felt something strong for his angel—yes, his angel—and if he hadn't planned to give up his place in Hell before, he certainly would have after meeting her. She inspired him, and being around her made him feel positive things. Things he had almost forgotten he had ever felt. Now he realized his decisions were going to get everyone around him hurt. It hadn't been his intention, but now the only thing he could do was face it.

"You are thinking too much," Lyla whispered in his ear as she kept her eyes open and her guard up.

"It is just strange. When I made the decision to leave Hell, I thought it would be me against the monsters. Now I fear it is going to end up hurting a lot of people who I never intended to hurt," Ashford answered as Piper, his daughter, started to stir in her bed.

"Our decisions always impact those around us, even if we don't intend it to. If you believe that your decision was the right one, then it was, and it will all work out as it is meant to," Lyla answered.

Becca had finished packing up the twins, and once again, Ashford had a twinge of fear. Piper left the bed and toddled over to him and Lyla. She looked up at Lyla as if she knew her, and of course, she did. The children always knew their guardian angel. Lyla picked her up and gave her a sweet hug.

Patrick wasn't quite ready to wake up, so Becca picked up the sleepy child and walked over to him. "I still have your number, if it is the same."

"It is," Ashford answered.

"I will text you all of their information. Please make sure you message me if you need anything." Becca handed his still mostly asleep son over to him.

"You might want to get out of here too for a while. Go somewhere safe like your Mom's or something till I get this fixed."

With the children in hand along with their things, he and Lyla turned to each other. "I'll meet you back in your room." He didn't think she knew yet that he was in the room next door.

Lyla nodded, and they teleported out.

Chapter 9

Lyla

"What were you thinking? You are supposed to be on vacation, and here you are not only working but bringing the children with you here?" Zimarra said right after Lyla and Ashford teleported into Lyla's room. Why was she even in her room?

Taking a deep breath, Lyla tried to think of the best way to explain, but there wasn't really a good answer. She had left to answer the call and then offered to help protect the kids while Ashford was under threats from his people. Lyla wasn't about to back down from the decision she made. "What was I supposed to do? The call woke me from my sleep. They are in real danger. I am doing what I am meant to do, and I won't apologize for that."

"Part of that is my fault. I needed her to help. Don't be angry with her." Ashford tried to calm the situation.

"No, not good enough. We are going to get in

so much trouble." Zimarra shook her head and took a seat on the bed.

Lyla set Piper down and manifested a toy for her to play with while Ashford laid Patrick down on the bed. Apparently, the boy was still tired. "I have a hard time believing that we would get in trouble for doing the right thing. Here, why don't we go outside and talk some?"

Lyla was sure Zimarra wouldn't understand everything, but she wanted to have a more one-on-one conversation with her friend. She headed out to the balcony. There had been some snow overnight, and it glistened a bit over the trees. This place never ceased to impress with the views.

"Lyla, I have never seen you go against any kind of orders. What is going one with you?" Zimarra asked, coming to stand next to her at the banister.

She was right. In all her time, Lyla had always stuck by all the rules. It was exactly how she had gotten in this position. Her need to always do the right thing, do her work, and be perfect had been what had made God send her on vacation. But was it possible the big man had put her where she was most needed? "I believe that everything happens for a reason. I was awakened with the call. I met Ashford who is the father of my charges. There has to be a reason all of this happened. I feel like something is happening."

Zimarra stood quietly for a while. She gazed out over the land as if deep in thought. "You have feelings for him. Like there is something that feels right with him?"

"I'm not sure. It certainly isn't like anything I have ever experienced before." Lyla took a deep breath.

"I understand how you feel. Trust me, I do. I also understand that it can make you want to do things you may not really want to do. He is a demon. As fun as enjoying time with him here on vacation might be, you can't lose sight of who you are. The last thing I would want to see is you fall." There was a sadness in her voice, as if her words held more experience than just advice. So many questions had been left unanswered when it came to what Zimarra did when she was away.

"I feel like you know so much more about all of this." Lyla leaned into her friend.

Snow began to fall, making a smile spread over Lyla's face. There wasn't a lot of snowfall, and it probably wouldn't stick. The flakes fluttered down from the sky. It was going to be a rather magical day.

"There are lots of things I have experienced that you don't know about. I just want you to be careful. Falling can be so tempting."

They stood there for a few moments before Lyla heard crying from inside the room. Apparently, Patrick had woken up and was a bit confused about where he was. Ashford stood there, seemingly lost with what to do. Lyla had a feeling he had never dealt with children before.

She saw the smile on Zimarra's face that matched hers.

Part of her wanted to wait and see what Ashford did. The other part of her wanted to go and save him from the stress. The two of them giggled for a moment while Ashford went to check on his son. Piper, on the other hand, didn't seem to be bothered by anything. Even after Ashford picked up the boy and tried to comfort him, the child continued to cry and wiggle, looking around frantically.

"I think I am going to go and save him. I have a feeling he doesn't have a lot of experience in this." Lyla stepped inside the room again and went over to Ashford. Her glow came up lightly, and the boy instantly calmed down. Reaching over, she grabbed one of the bags and grinned. "I think he needs his diaper changed, and they are probably both hungry. I will call and see if we can get some room service sent up.

"How do you know this?" Ashford whispered.

"Well, it is what I do. I have been taking care of children for all of my existence. I may have picked up on a few things."

"I'm not sure I remember any of my existence before the fall. I'm glad you are here."

Lyla watched as he looked at the diaper and wipes, once again confused. "Here, let me show you how to do this. But you do need to learn. They are your children, and I may not always be there when they need a change."

With a bit of a chuckle, Lyla went about showing Ashford what to do. It took everything in her to not laugh when he turned a bit green. Well, there was always a starting point for everyone. Lyla had no doubt that, with time, he would get the hang of things. Once Patrick was put back together, they checked on Piper. This time, Ashford tried out his fatherly skills at changing her while Lyla called room service. A smile lit up his face, and pride beamed from him as he completed his work.

Lyla was surprised by Ashford with every moment they spent together. She had always carried preconceived notions about how demons acted. When they had met, she expected him to be conceited and arrogant with a tinge of evil. Now she knew better. Though he was confident, she had yet to see him be vicious or vile. No, just funny and flirty. It warmed her, and she realized just what Zimarra had been talking about.

Her friend knew, somehow, just how easily it would be to get caught in the charm of someone like Ashford. It made her warning ring with undeniable truth. Part of Lyla wanted to ignore the caution. The desire she felt toward Ashford, especially now, seeing him with the kids, was strong and pulled at her in ways she never thought to experience. It was a beautiful feeling, almost as strong and fulfilling as what she felt when she did her work.

"Hey, I am going to go down to the desk and let

them know about the two extra guests. Maybe they have some little beds or something for them. You two behave." Zimarra walked toward the door, a knowing look on her face.

"Thank you so much, Zimarra. You have no idea how much this means to me," Lyla said, walking with her and giving her friend a hug before she walked out of the room.

Alone, Lyla didn't know what to say. It seemed Ashford was at a loss, too, as he watched her, a confused look on his face. "Well, now that I have them here, I have no idea what to do."

"How much of your power did they inherit?" Lyla asked, coming over to sit next to him on the bed.

"Honestly, I have no idea. I haven't seen them since just after they were born. I didn't want them to suffer because of who and what I was. My hope was if I stepped away from them then maybe they would be safe," Ashford answered. "When I told Becca the truth, she was furious. Honestly, I worried she was going to want to give them up, but she just wanted me out of their lives. We agreed that it was best."

"And now you have to protect them." Lyla arched a brow, wanting to understand more about their situation.

"Yeah, well, apparently, no matter how much you do to keep the ones you care about safe, eventually something may still happen. I never told anyone about them. I stayed away. I only had a few pictures of them from when they were born. I let my guard down for one minute, and now they are in a huge amount of danger. Everything I did, everything I gave up was for nothing." It was apparent Ashford was bitter about his sacrifice.

"Sadly, all we can do is be there and hope it is enough. So long as the ones we love know we are there for them and doing all we can for them, then they have the best tools." Lyla gave him a smile, and his body relaxed. "Now, after we eat, how about we see if they handle the cold well? If so, we can take them out to the lazy river."

Chapter 10

Lyla

B reakfast had been nice, and the kids had done well with eating their cereal. Even though danger loomed over them, Lyla felt it best they try to keep the children as happy and entertained as possible. The children at least had Ashford's ability to withstand extreme temperatures, which was perfect. With the light snow falling, it was a beautiful day to enjoy floating along in the lazy river.

Lyla and Ashford had gotten a boat-like float for the little ones to play in. Enough water had come in for the two of them to splash around but not enough to put them at risk. Then they had tied the boat to both of their inner tubes to prevent them from getting away from the two of them. All of them had drinks, and the music playing set a happy mood.

Relaxing back in her inner tube, she smiled up at the beauty of the towering redwoods surrounding the resort. Now and then, she stuck out her tongue to catch random snowflakes as they fell. The kids tried to catch the frozen crystals between splashes in the water. Ashford lay in his tube with his eyes closed, breathing shallowly. Lyla had known he was more than exhausted. They had a long night, and his was even longer trying to stay up to watch the twins while they slept. She was sure he hadn't gotten any sleep.

So, while they floated around the lazy river, she let Ashford get a little rest, and she kept all her senses on high alert for any threats which might come their way. It was the least she could do, and she was enjoying it. They enjoyed floating around the river for some time. All the while, Lyla thought about all that had happened to her since meeting Ashford the day before. With the strong emotions she had for him and the way Ashford seemed to want to redeem himself from his life in Hell, it was hard for her to turn away. Well, he hadn't said he wanted to redeem himself, so she needed to be cautious not to get too attached to that line of thinking. Still his actions had made her believe it was his intention.

Sure, it was probably best for her to just leave it be and go back to her life in Heaven after she enjoyed her vacation, but she knew deep down part of her being on vacation at this time, at this resort, was because of the man sleeping in the water next to her. Lyla could not turn her back on what she felt and what she knew in her heart to be true. Try as she might, there was no denying it.

Her friend had made it clear Lyla should be cautious, and for the first time in all her existence, Lyla had no desire at all to play it safe. Strange, for the longest time, Lyla had been the one warning Zimarra to be more careful, and now it was the other way around. Lyla needed to talk with her friend again. She wanted her opinion and feedback on the decision she was making.

As difficult as it was for her to let go of her guard, it was more difficult for her to turn her back on what was right. Looking around and seeing the two children splashing and playing in the water boat made it all worth it. The warmth it gave her had her smiling. Yes, she was willing to give in to her emotions and feelings, knowing it also meant they would be safe. However, there was still a nagging feeling inside of her, making her feel uneasy.

Or was that the feeling of someone watching them? Looking around, she tried to find where the energy was coming from. No one other than some of the other guests she had seen the day before and resort staff members was around. Of course, there was a possibility one of those people had been working for those after Ashford all along.

Pulling the boat closer to her, she sent her senses out a little more, trying to seek out any danger. With all the different types of supernaturals there, it was hard to decipher if there was a threat or not. Ashford groaned a bit, and the way he shifted had her worried he was going to fall out of the float. He managed to keep his balance as he blinked his eyes open. Lyla saw the strain it took for him to pull himself out of his sleep, and part of her wanted to tell him to get more rest. However, she was sure he was ready to be awake and face the day.

"How long have I been asleep?" Ashford asked, turning to look toward them.

"A little over an hour, but we were having so much fun I didn't see the point in waking you. Do you feel any better?"

"Everyone is going to have prunes for fingers." Ashford chuckled, looking at his own hands to confirm. "I feel as good as I can having been stabbed and then not slept. So, I guess that is the best answer I can give you."

"Well, I will take it. I think we should head back inside, maybe have some lunch, and let these two get a nap. Besides, I feel like I can narrow down what is going on when I am not in such an open space," Lyla explained before diving into the water so she could pull them toward the edge where the stairs were.

"Good idea. I'm pretty sure nap time was somewhere on that list of what I'm supposed to do with the kids." Ashford got out of the inner tube to help get the kids out of the lazy river and take them inside.

***

Ashford

Lyla was an utter pro with the kids. To be honest, Ashford wasn't sure if he would have been able to do this without her. It didn't help that he was starting to feel things for her he never thought he would have for anyone. Sure, he had met others he had feelings for, but it was superficial. What he had building inside of him was deep and pure. Strange because he was sure nothing in his life would ever be pure again.

Leaning against the dresser in the room, he watched as she finished putting the kids to bed. She had sat there and sang to them until both children were asleep. With the kids tucked in, she came closer to him. "I felt like someone was watching us while we were at the pool, but I couldn't pinpoint anything."

Ashford was pretty sure he had felt something, which was what had woken him up. Like Lyla, he hadn't seen anyone nor could he pinpoint anything, but there was something there. "Yeah, I think I did too. They aren't going to stop, especially now that I have them with me. The kids are a liability, but not having them, like I said before, put them in even more danger. They are going to try and be stealthy, so we will need to stay on our toes."

"It isn't like they have been out in the open so far as it is. They got you with a surprise attack at the party then cornered you when you were alone in your room. I have a feeling they don't have any plans to give up their position." Lyla leaned her head against Ashford's shoulder.

"You shouldn't be staying with me, you know. I'm going to be nothing but trouble for you." Ashford placed his head against hers.

"Maybe, but I'm here, and I'm not going anywhere. So, get used to it. Besides, we are in my room," Lyla answered, a chuckle following as she turned and kissed his cheek.

Ashford didn't say anything else. He turned into Lyla's somewhat innocent kiss and took control. He pressed his lips to hers and picked up where their kiss had left off the night before. Once again, he found himself intoxicated by the taste of her. It had him pulling her into him, pressing their bodies more heatedly together. Through it, he could feel the pounding of her heart against his chest. His fingers itching to make more of the moment, Ashford was so lost in his time with her he didn't even realize they were no longer alone.

"Now, isn't that cute." a female voice said, breaking their focus on each other and drawing it toward her.

Chapter 11

Ashford

S lowly, Ashford turned toward the speaker. Cassandra stood leaning against the door to the balcony. The look on her face said it all. She had no doubt her presence in the room put her in a position of power. Of course, there was no way she knew about Lyla and who and what she was. Lyla changed everything. When Cassandra figured it out, it would be too late. Well, that was the hope at least.

He pushed away from the dresser and moved cautiously and confidently toward her. "And what is that, Cass?"

"So, I see you have decided to bring all your eggs into one basket. Did you really think bringing the babes closer to you would keep them safer? I would think, after all this time, you would know better. Try as you might, unless you give in to me and go back home, no one in your life is safe." Cassandra laughed, evil dripping in her tone.

"That is where you are wrong. I have lived in that world long enough to know all of your tricks. Try all you want, but I'm not going back unless you kill me. And you aren't going to hurt anyone in this room, because I have no qualms with destroying you and anyone else who thinks it might be a good idea to come after me."

"Bravado isn't going to save you, Ashford. What are you going to do? Fight me along with your little girlfriend over there? I don't care what she is, she can't help you, and you certainly can't take me on your own." Cassandra moved in closer, getting right in Ashford's face.

"I will break you. Don't test me. Just because you're the new favorite doesn't make you better than me." Ashford growled, getting so close to her face he could feel the heat of her breath on his cheek.

"Like I said, isn't that cute. I have earned my place, and I don't need your validation. You are a has-been, and when you get home, you are going to rot away in torture, and I am going to keep rising in the ranks. You, on the other hand, well, you said you wanted to retire." There was a sexy sound to the woman's voice, but Ashford knew it was really venom.

He couldn't wait around for something to just happen, and the banter was getting old. Ashford reached out, taking hold of Cassandra's shoulders before delivering a massive headbutt. The action sent the woman back, stunning her, which allowed him the chance to get a few more incredibly powerful strikes in. He hit her hard with his elbow, driving the point to the top of her head, then swiped her legs out from underneath her, sending her flying onto her back. He tried to drop his knees into her chest, but he missed when she rolled backward landing onto her feet, agile like a cat.

For a moment, her eyes filled with flame almost as dark as the blood pouring from her broken nose from Ashford's headbutt, and she flung her hand out, sending a force of power in Ashford's direction. Try as he might, he couldn't get out of the way fast enough, and it sent him flying into a mirror, shattering the glass all over the floor. The sound of children crying filled the air, but Ashford couldn't let that distract him. If he lost focus, he wouldn't have any babies to fight for. He focused on Cassandra and raced forward again, his own eyes ablaze with power.

The two of them crashed into each other, an eruption of power bursting from them as their fight evolved from more than just mere hitting, kicking, and blocking expertly to hitting, kicking, and blocking with enough power and speed that any one shot would have shattered a mortal. While their hand-to-hand combat was quite impressive, the burst of energy behind each movement really made it shine. He slammed into her, igniting fire into his palm strike, and sent her soaring across the room. Cassandra returned with a slicing kick to his cheek that left a three-inch gash across his face and dropped him to one knee. His demonic blood had it healing quickly.

That was the problem with their kind fighting. Neither of them could really hurt each other without something specifically meant to do so. Ashford knew Cassandra had those tools. She had already used them against him before, and he wouldn't put it past her to use them again. Cassandra proved his suspicion right when she manifested two blades and held them out pointed down for him to see. There was no mistaking the sickly drip of poison, a poison meant to kill other demons, tainting both knives. It had been what she used against him before. If not for Lyla, he would have already died.

"I'm tired of pussyfooting around. It is time to get serious. Give up now, or I kill you all." Cassandra growled and crouched ready to strike.

Blue light filled the room, blinding Ashford, and he couldn't see Cassandra anymore. For a moment, he panicked, worried the other demon would be able to get past the light and to him before he could react. However, when his eyes started to clear, he saw Lyla. She had two crescent-shaped blades in her hands and had charged forward. Cassandra cowered in fear, weakened by the angelic energy. In the background, the children had quieted. Something about her power soothed them. It, however, didn't soothe him or make Cassandra feel very well.

The other demon jumped up and tried to attack Lyla. Their blades clashed together repeatedly, creating a spark of unearthly energy so fast the clanking of metal on metal was almost a constant high-pitched ringing. The longer Cassandra was in Lyla's aura, the weaker she became. Ashford knew this because he too felt it happening. He knew the moment Cassandra realized she was in over her head. Her angry eyes glared over at him a moment before she ported away, and Lyla stumbled forward.

For several excruciatingly long moments, Ashford basked in the beauty and glory of Lyla's high angelic form. It was epic in magnitude compared to her aura and use of power at Becca's house earlier. He had not been in such presence since the fall, and no amount of pain or weakness could take away from how incredible she looked standing before him. All too soon, the power faded, and Lyla ran over to check on him. Her warm hand against his cheek made every nerve in his body tingle with life, and without thinking about it, he pulled her onto him and began to kiss her once more.

Their kisses always got interrupted. It had started to become a point of great frustration for him. Now after such an exhilarating burst of holy power, Ashford needed something to ground him. When Lyla opened to his kiss, he took that as an invitation to really enjoy her. He shifted enough to have her sitting on his lap and ran his hand up her back, sinking his fingers into her hair and twisting just enough so he had a light hold on her. The soft sound she made when he did it surprised him. Ashford wasn't even sure she realized she had done it.

The kiss grew from that though. He deepened it, feeding from her mouth like a starving madman. In all his life, he had never felt such intensity when with someone. Sure, there had been nights full of passion and pleasure but nothing with the raw amorous drive he felt for Lyla. It was as if he would stop his whole life just to be with her. It certainly made him no longer want to give up and die. However, he knew, in the end, he couldn't be what he was and be with her.

No! He refused to let himself think about that. Not when he had her in his arms, wrapped in his body. Her warmth made him feel like he had gone home, and he wanted nothing more than to bask in it for the rest of the night. Putting up a barrier that blocked sound and vision between them and where the children were sleeping, he let his hands roam over her body, feeling her curves. Lyla tensed, and when she did, he felt her pull away.

"Don't be afraid. I swear I'm not going to hurt you. I just want to be with you." Ashford wasn't sure if he sounded like an idiot or not, but he had to give it a try. Sure, Lyla probably had no experience, but it didn't mean she couldn't gain some. Unless the rules had changed since The Great Fall.

Lyla pulled away enough that she could look into his eyes. His hands still rested on the curve of her waist, and he could feel how heavy her breaths came. Her eyes were filled with bright blue light, making him feel a sense of hope and belonging he hadn't in a long time. "I want to believe that isn't true, but you're a demon. What happens...?"

"When I'm with you, I'm just Ashford. I don't want to be this any longer. I just want to be with you and keep my family safe." He kept his answer short as he then pulled her in for another intense kiss. This time, there was far more emotion to it. Pain pounded through his chest, almost like his heart was breaking, or maybe, for the first time in a long time, the broken pieces were being put back together. Either way, he knew it was love, and no matter what happened, he would never want to let her go. Not without a fight.

Chapter 12

Lyla

Lyla wasn't sure she could explain the feeling she had inside of her. It was a mix of pain and longing she had never known was possible. All her life, she had lived to serve. She served God, her children, and her purpose to the fullest. There had never been time for her to think of anything else. Let alone feel anything else. This feeling she had now tingled deep inside of her and had her body heated. It made her long to touch Ashford in ways that didn't seem right, yet somehow, they did.

Despite what humans thought, angels were not all celibate beings of pureness. They were allowed to enjoy some of the pleasures of life, so long as they did their service to God. It was something she had always done before and something she valued in herself. Part of the reason she never gave in to more normal aspects of life was because she felt it would ultimately take her away from her duty. However, she couldn't pull away from

Ashford. There was a force pulling them together, and no matter what she felt or the two of them thought, she couldn't bring herself to stop it.

The more she kissed him, the more she realized just how lonely and sad her life really was without someone to share it with. In a way, it had never been completely fulfilled, but she had never realized it until just that moment. Her arms wrapped more tightly around him, and she drew him closer to her. She felt so good having his heat pressed to her. It made her cry out, which in turn made her blush.

"Don't be embarrassed. I love hearing you enjoy yourself," Ashford whispered against her lips before moving his kisses along her cheek and jaw. "You taste so good. I don't think I will ever get enough of you."

Her breathing became labored the more he kissed her, and she barely noticed when his hands moved under the hem of her shirt to press his fingertips against her bare skin. The sensation of it all was just far too good to ignore. Dizzy and lost to the power of it all, she said nothing when he lifted her in his arms and placed her on the bed. All her friend's warnings and all her own warnings were gone. She longed to be with this man, this demon, more than anything. Maybe, just maybe, the two of them being together could save him from all that seemed bent on destroying him.

"You are thinking too much. Relax. Enjoy." Ashford moaned, his hand running the length of her body and down her leg before riding back up and under her bottom.

Lyla didn't have an answer for that, so she didn't try. Instead, she did the best she could to calm her racing thoughts and enjoy the sensation of his hands and lips and body. Feeling brave, Lyla let her hands roam, and without thinking about it, her fingers explored under his shirt. The warmth of his skin sent jolts of sensation through her body, tightening something low in her. The pressure was a lot for her to handle and she rocked her body against him. A pleasurable sound came from Ashford. She smiled. Had she done that?

As if reading her and knowing what she wanted, he began to move along with her. He pushed up her shirt, revealing more and more of her skin, until it pushed up over her chest. Something about revealing more of herself to him relaxed her. She thought it would make her nervous, but no, it made her feel powerful and strong. It also made her feel sexy and cared for.

Not wanting to waste any of the buildup, Lyla began to pull at his clothes too. She had made her decision. The pull between the two of them was too intense, and she wanted to see what happened with them. She helped strip off his clothes as he did with hers. It wasn't rushed. They took their time, exploring each other as they removed each article of clothing. When they were both completely naked, Lyla basked in the feel of the warmth of Ashford's flesh pressed fully against hers.

"You are the most beautiful woman I have ever seen," Ashford whispered, delivering kiss after kiss along her chest.

"Thank you. You are as well." Lyla didn't know what to say. Part of her felt like what she said was stupid, but Ashford didn't let her dwell on it as he came in for another deep kiss. He lifted his body and moved his hand between them, his fingers searching for that nub of pressure between her legs.

Lyla cried out as he softly began to stroke her, taking his time at first before building to a faster speed and more intensity. She found herself wiggling and moving, not sure how to react to what was happening. It felt like she was nearing an edge yet also desperate for release. She chanted please as her hips rose and fell, trying to seek out some sort of release from the tension. This seemed to please Ashford as he growled, and she felt the vibration the entire length of her body.

"Just a little more. I want to feel you. See you." His purr tingled to her very core, and her panting grew heavier with each swift stroke of his finger.

Lyla was sure she would go mad if she had to endure much more. As if her body realized her predicament, it let go of everything, exploding out into a force of pure ecstasy. Light radiated from her, basking the room in a cool blue hue and making Ashford hiss. She didn't really notice it. All she could do was feel and ride out wave after wave of pleasure. Just when she thought she was coming down from it all, Ashford shifted, and she cried out once more as her body was filled. His pulsing hardness intensified her bliss tenfold.

Their arms and legs once again wrapped tightly around each other, and she scraped her nails down his back as he began to slowly ride in and out of her. Together, they continued this dance of passion and something deeper. She could feel his heart as if it were her own, and she longed to make it better. It made her cling tighter to him, kiss him with greater desire, and do all she could to make love to him. No longer did her ignorance of the act matter. Her heart and body knew what to do when it came to him. She cherished him like nothing else, and in that moment, as they were one, he was all that mattered.

Each moment built upon the last. She was not sure how long the two of them were tangled together before the coil inside of her began to build once more. She felt him inside of her, growing and pulsing harder, and it had her crying out. Gazing deep into his fiery eyes, she saw his longing and need, and the moment their lips melded together once more, the two of them exploded together. Every nerve in her body sang out in joy at what they had shared.

They lay there for several long moments just basking in one another. Neither one wanted to let go and face the reality they lived in. No, she wanted to simply be with him, hold him, and let him know everything was going to be fine, but she couldn't promise that. It was foolish to even think that. Instead, the two of them lay there, holding each other and pretending the rest of the world didn't exist.

Chapter 13

Ashford

He woke with his nose buried against her neck. Her hair had scattered across his cheek, and the sweet scent of her skin made his mouth water with desire. They had stayed up most of the night, making love over and over until they couldn't stay awake any longer.

In his mind, Ashford heard Aerosmith singing. The sweet melody rang true because he surely didn't want to miss a moment with Lyla. It was pure bliss lying there with her in his arms, and it gave him a sense of serenity he hadn't felt in a very long time.

If only it could last.

Unfortunately, the dangers chasing him were not going to simply vanish just because he had finally found happiness. If anything, it would just get worse. As much as he wanted to savor every moment he could with her, deep down, he knew their night together was only a short reprieve before his inevitable demise.

Lyla couldn't save him. No one could. He had made his choice to leave Hell with a double middle-finger salute, and the grand demon lords were not happy about it. Ashford knew too much and had risen too high in the ranks. It wasn't like he was some peon demon no one gave two shits about.

Anger stirred inside of him, and he pulled Lyla tighter against him. She had been his calm in this storm—the sweet salvation he had always looked for—and it sucked that it would all be ending so quickly. As skilled of a warrior as Ashford was, he was no match for what would be coming next.

The shrill shriek of a very unhappy baby pulled Ashford out of his little pity party, and he pried himself away from Lyla so he could check on the kids. They had slept well, and he was pretty sure it had something to do with whatever magic Lyla had used on them to keep them safe from Cassandra.

"I'm not sure I have ever slept that good." Lyla groaned from the bed a few moments before she pulled the covers off so she could get up.

Just the sight of those sweet curves naked against the mattress got his blood going again. If not for the kids, he would have surely jumped her for another round. He savored watching her get up and stretch before putting her clothes on. Her fingers combed through her silky blonde hair, giving it a gentle toss, and Ashford grinned at the fact that, even after all their vigorous activity, she still looked perfect.

When they were both dressed, he put the shield down so they could check the little ones.

"Why don't you go in and order up some breakfast, and I will get the kids cleaned up?" Lyla suggested as she moved over to Patrick who was in the most distress.

"I can do that." Ashford picked up the phone and made the order, doing his best to remember what Lyla liked as well as the kids.

When he turned around, no one was in the room. It took him a second for his heart rate to slow before he heard running water. Sure enough, with a quick investigation of the bathroom, he saw Lyla was giving the twins a bath. With a wave of her hand, toys manifested in the tub for them to play with and bubbles quickly enveloped the little ones.

While they were distracted playing, Lyla went about washing hair, faces, and little bodies until they were all nice and clean. Ashford still couldn't believe how easy it came for the angel.

"Oh, hey, grab some towels. Let's get them dressed before breakfast gets here, but just in something we don't care if it gets dirty."

Ashford did as Lyla asked, bringing over two fluffy towels. She handed Patrick over to him then lifted Piper up and wrapped her in a second towel. They took the two back into the bedroom and diapered and dressed them in onesies for breakfast before setting them in their highchairs.

"I'm going to find a way to help you," Lyla said.

Ashford turned toward her, everything about him getting more stoic. "There is no saving me. I made my choices, and I have to pay the price for them. I thought I could do it, stay safe and keep them out of it, but the longer I try to fight this, the more danger I'm putting everyone else in."

"That is a defeatist way of looking at things. There is always a way to win. I have seen that in you. What changed?" Lyla sounded angry, a tone Ashford hadn't heard from her yet.

"I just don't want them, or you, to get hurt just because of what I chose to do." There was obvious frustration in Ashford's voice, even though he tried to hold it back. He knew Lyla wanted to help, but Ashford was a realist. His choices were going to be the end of him. All he really wanted now was to enjoy the little bit of time he had with Lyla and his children.

"They are not going to get hurt, not as long as I am around, and I am no weakling in need of saving. I am more than capable of fighting and taking care of not only myself but all of you. Please don't imply otherwise."

The fire in her voice was not something he expected. Despite his desire to continue to argue with her, he grinned a moment before he wrapped his arms around her and pulled her toward him to give her a heated kiss.

"I have no idea how you have so much faith,"

Ashford whispered against her lips. It was a bit of a silly question; after all, angels were meant to have faith. However, it was still difficult for him to believe it, no matter who said it.

"Well, you can think and believe what you want. And you can kiss me to try and distract me, but I mean every word of what I am saying,"

They were interrupted by the knocking of room service at the door. Ashford went to collect their breakfast and worked with Lyla to set it out on the table. The children giggled upon seeing the shamrock-shaped pancakes on the plate. Lyla helped to get their pancakes cut up, and she and Ashford helped the kids eat while they ate. The food was amazing, and the coffee was even better. Having a few minutes to relax and be away from the conversation of his impending demise had been exactly what he needed.

They had just started cleaning up their breakfast when there was a loud pounding at the door. They looked at one another, intense curiosity crossing their faces. Cautiously, Ashford approached the door while Lyla took up a protective stance between the door and the children. He glanced over his shoulder to make sure Lyla was ready and then opened the door.

Zimarra pushed through, a frantic look on her face. "Where is Lyla?"

Chapter 14

Lyla

L yla watched as Ashford stumbled back and her best friend burst through the door to her room. Her face was a mix of anger and worry, and her eyes were ablaze with angelic fury. The wild angel searched the room enraged and ready for a fight until her eyes finally fell on Lyla. By that point, Lyla had calmed down, an amused smile falling over her face. Usually, it was Lyla who was on edge and worried about Zimarra, not the other way around.

"What happened in here? I have been worried sick about you all night!" Zimarra rushed over and wrapped her arms around Lyla. Warmth unlike anything else soaked into her. There was nothing quite like the protective aura of a guardian angel. It wasn't just the ethereal light that had Lyla heated. Zimarra's question sent a deep flush over Lyla.

Heart pounding and a bit of sweat forming on her palms, she pulled away and gave Zimarra what she thought was a smile. By the look on her friend's face, Lyla was pretty sure it wasn't as sweet and smooth as she had anticipated. Rage built back up in her friend's eyes a moment before she swung around and charged Ashford. The demon was caught so off guard that he was tackled easily.

"How dare you! How dare you do that to her! She deserves better than you!" Zimarra screeched as she pounded into Ashford.

To his credit, Ashford just put his arms up to block Zimarra instead of fighting back and hurting her.

"Stop it! Ashford didn't do anything wrong. Believe it or not, I am capable of making my own choices. Now get off of him!" Lyla reached down and pulled her rabid friend off Ashford. For all the encouragement Zimarra had given Lyla to flirt and have fun with Ashford, she certainly didn't like the progression the relationship was taking. When she turned her so the two of them were face to face, what she saw was something she hadn't expected. Zimarra almost looked heartbroken.

"I know you can make your own choices, but you have no idea what you have done. Trust me, this doesn't end well." Zimarra marched out of the room, slamming the door closed.

Ashford carefully rose from the floor and dusted himself off. Lyla hadn't realized just how badly her body was shaking until he wrapped his arms around her and pulled her into him. Soft, calming sounds filled the air as Ashford, who had just been attacked by her best friend, whispered and hummed in an attempt to make her feel better. It didn't seem right, but she refused to push him away. The comfort he gave her instantly relieved her anxiety and distress.

"I'm sorry she did that to you," Lyla whispered against his chest. The muffled sound made her wonder if he even heard her.

"Don't worry about it. Zimarra is being protective of you, and I can't be angry at her for that. I'm trying to do the same thing," Ashford whispered. His lips pressed into the top of her head, and a flood of emotion pounded out for Lyla's heart.

They stood there in that warm embrace, basking in the intense emotion building higher and higher between them. One Lyla could only describe as love, even if she was not willing to admit it. As they held each other, Lyla tried to make sense of what Zimarra said. What had happened to her friend to make her so angry about Lyla spending a night with Ashford? Had she fallen in love with a demon before, and had it not gone well? No, that didn't seem right at all. Maybe she had just fallen in love before. The idea of her best friend walking around with a broken heart and having never told her saddened Lyla. How could she be a good friend if she didn't know?

Giggles and the playful clattering of dishes broke the almost spell the two of them had been in. When they turned toward the twins, Lyla laughed as she saw a food fight seemed to have emerged between them. "Well, so much for that bath."

"Yeah, next time, we wait until after we feed them." Ashford chuckled and headed for the table to break up the sticky war. "All right, all right. I know the two of you have warrior blood, but come on. Pancakes are not weapons; they are food. Warriors need food to keep their strength."

His words had Lyla laughing as she walked over to help him. Together, they cleaned up the dining area and cleaned and dressed the twins.

***

Two days had passed. Two joyous days spent with the children, and two nights spent making love, but the children were getting restless. There was only so much to do in the rooms, and the children had been cooped up for too long. They decided to take the kids for a walk and trust in her guardian powers to warn them of any immediate danger. The day had turned out a little warmer than expected, and the fresh air was sure to do everyone a little good. Lyla and Ashford found a nice spot to stop and let the kids play, so they laid out a blanket and let the little ones toddle around with a few toys. Lyla sat close to Ashford, leaning against him. Her hope was that her feelings for him would soak into him and he would stop being so stubborn.

Daytime seemed to be when they had the most peace. Maybe the demons only came out at night, or maybe they just got lucky. No, luck didn't have anything to do with it. "Why do the demons only seem to attack at night?" Lyla asked, curious if there was a reason. Maybe it would be something they could use to prevent being snuck up on again.

"Our power is stronger at night, but that doesn't mean we have to wait for nightfall to come out, obviously. It is also just how we usually work. I don't think anyone down there has thought about the idea of attacking me during the day. Of course, with how badly Cassandra failed, I'm pretty sure we won't be seeing her next. There is going to be someone else next. Someone we are not going to like," Ashford answered.

"Who do you think is coming next?" Lyla shifted so she could better look at him while they talked.

"Lyla, I have already told you I'm not going to get you any more involved than you already are. Can't we just enjoy this time we have? I don't think I have ever been happier in my life, and I want to savor it. The last thing I want to do is talk about what is coming or how everything is going to turn out." Ashford leaned down to give her a sweet and passionate kiss.

She couldn't deny their time together was magical. She certainly would rather snuggle with Ashford, watch the kids, and then go out dancing with him when the sun set. However, the truth was, they had some dangerous enemies after them, and it was only a matter of time before they came for them once more. They didn't have the luxury of simply enjoying each other, but soon they would. Lyla was sure of it, even if Ashford wasn't.

Nearby, the children continued to laugh and play, oblivious to the dangers of the world and the kisses she and Ashford shared. Lyla could feel her heart grow more and more full with every one, as if there had been a void there she never knew existed. In that small little patch of grass, they were something special. She hadn't even realized her glow came upon her until Ashford moaned against her lips and pulled her closer. Her aura didn't seem to hurt him any longer. If anything, he basked in it like a desperate man in search of comfort, and she was more than happy to provide that.

Their bubble away from the world popped when Piper screamed and Patrick cried. Ashford and Lyla jerked their heads to see what had happened just as a tall man with long pointy blond hair disappeared with the children in a mass of shadows.

Chapter 15

Ashford

A shford jumped in an attempt to reach his children before M'Kal got away with them, but he wasn't fast enough to reach the demon baron. No, they were gone, and it was his fault. He had told Becca they would be safer with him, but he had been wrong. Now they were in more danger than he could have ever imagined. Rage boiled in him like a furnace ready to blow, and he roared. Come for him, hurt him, but don't take his children. It had been all he asked, all he cared about.

From the start, he knew his fate. The moment he left Hell, he had known what that would mean for him. He never imagined it would mean his children would be taken from him. Hotter and more volatile he became until a gentle hand pressed against his shoulder. Almost instantly he could think again, breathe again. Though he was still angry, he no longer saw red.

"We will get them back," Lyla whispered in a

soft voice as her body pressed in behind him, holding him for a moment. Once again, her soft blue light came to surround the two of them, and he soaked it in like rays of sunlight. It didn't hurt; it gave him strength and calm. It helped him focus when all he wanted to do was act with rage and haste. For as many times as he had crossed paths with angels before, never had one's aura helped him rather than hurt him.

"What is happening to me?" Ashford sighed, leaning into her and taking in the sensation of her protective light. He hadn't even realized she had taken them back to the room.

"I'm not sure, but let's not question it. We have bigger things to worry about. So, let's get moving. Who was that guy, and where can we find him?" He could feel her determination and desire to help him. Her voice held a steel edge of resolve that cut through his worry and self-hate, and it helped pull him out of his feelings enough to think.

M'Kal had come for him himself. That wasn't typical. After all, demon barons had better things to do with their time than chase down rogues. It was why Cassandra had been sent. Sure, she had failed, but Ashford figured they would just send someone else. The fact M'Kal came instead of sending someone in proxy meant something— and not in the mushy sort of way.

"He was my former employer. I worked for M'Kal, doing his bidding, when I was down in Hell. He was a powerful warrior, ruthless and dedicated, so much so that after his accomplishments in the original war between Heaven and Hell he was made a baron. It was an honor only a handful of fallen were lucky enough to have bestowed upon them. So, when I left, M'Kal was the one I threw the middle finger at. He is the one who has been sending Cassandra after me. I guess, after that didn't work, he decided to take things into his own hands."

Ashford drew in a deep breath before continuing. "I was an enforcer for M'Kal. While he held a portion of Hell, much like a lord of the land would, I was his trusty proverbial knight. When a soul was beyond what a normal demon could handle or when a battle was versus a powerful opponent, I was the one who stepped in. It was always on M'Kal's order, and it was always brutal. M'Kal enjoyed his torture more than most. If he took my kids, there is no telling what he is going to do to them."

Ashford couldn't bring himself to look Lyla in the eyes. Confessing his purpose in Hell to her brought him nothing short of irrevocable shame. He didn't deserve her or her help, even if she had made it clear she wouldn't take no for an answer.

"You are valuable to him. I can understand that. I'm sure there are things you know that other demons don't, so you are dangerous to him. It is possible he also took your leaving personally. However, if he is as bad as you say and you were no longer happy, I can understand you wanting to leave. It should be your choice if you stay or go. Wasn't that the whole point of the fall after all." Lyla whispered, turning him so she could kiss his cheek. The warmth of it exploded inside of him, stirring a part of him he thought long dead.

"Demons don't get a choice. It is what it is. Our choice was to fall, and after that, we became slaves to the masters in Hell. Had I known then what I know now, I would never have given up my place. Had I known we were to become monsters who led men astray just to torture them, I would never have made the greatest mistake of my life." Ashford felt as if his heart was shattered.

The sensation of Lyla's aura made him remember all he had given up, and for what? To turn around and be someone else's lackey? It had not been what they had been promised when they all took that leap. They had been told they would have freedom and power. Sure, he had power, but its use belonged to someone else.

"It has been a very long time, and wallowing in the past only makes taking care of the current situation that much harder. You know M'Kal. So, how do we get to him?" Lyla asked, bringing him out of his single-person pity party.

"Well, if we can help it, we don't want to fight him on his own ground. Normally, innocent children could not be taken to Hell, they are innately pure, but with my demonic blood, I fear that's the first place he would take them. Demons are more powerful in Hell, and it is even more true for the barons, as they don't leave Hell that often.

"I don't know if my former master took my kids as revenge for leaving, as a bargaining chip to make me return, or to prevent me from sharing information I accumulated working for him— information M'Kal thinks is dangerous to him. Not that it matters. As long as he is in Hell and has the twins, they are in danger. We need to think of a way to get him up here. Maybe…"

He paused as an idea hit him. Masters wanted power and often were willing to make deals. Bargaining and deals were like currency in Hell. If Ashford could offer M'Kal something the baron simply could not refuse, he might be able to lure him back out of Hell and onto neutral ground.

"Lyla, do you trust me?" Ashford asked, pulling her hands in front of her and holding them tight. It was a loving gesture, and he did all he could to send that emotion into her.

Ashford watched as a play of emotions raced behind his sweet angel's eyes. He couldn't blame her for being cautious. After all, despite how bonded they were growing, he was still a demon. However, he needed her to trust him in this. It was more important than nearly anything else, because if she could fully give him her trust, then he might be able take out M'Kal and save his children.

Lyla licked her lips, and her eyes locked to his, gazing deeply into him. He got the feeling she was trying to read him or gather some sort of information. His heart pounded like a bass drum at a rock concert, and dizziness enveloped him as his breath grew heavy. "Yes, I trust you."

Ashford wasn't sure if any words had ever felt or sounded so good. An explosion of emotion took over him, and he pulled her into him for a deep and passionate kiss. Yes, they had work to do, but first, he had to savor those words, that moment, and bask in the glory of the woman before him. No one trusted demons. Certainly, no angel did. The proof had been evident in how Zimarra had treated him. But Lyla trusted him. She had given him the one thing he had always wanted, and he was grateful for it.

Their kiss grew more and more heated, and had they not been in the midst of a crisis, he would have thrown her down on the bed and ravished her body until she was screaming for him. Too bad they didn't have time for that. Instead, he pulled away, panting and gasping for air. Lyla's cheeks were flushed, and her eyes held a glazed look, showing she had been just as consumed by their passion. Chuckling, he took one last moment of pleasure from their kiss, and her loss of control from just one kiss made him proud of himself. He pulled away, still holding tightly to her hands.

"I think I have fallen again," Ashford whispered, looking down at her dainty wrist and summoning up some of his power. "I think I may now become a slave to you, but first, do your best and remember that you trust me."

He manifested a pair of manacles around her wrists. He watched as she gasped and nearly collapsed into his arms. The enchantment in the cuffs blocked her angelic power. They had been created by the demon princes to hunt down angels and slaughter them during the war of the fallen. Ashford had never used them before; he had never had a reason to. Watching the weakness consume Lyla broke his heart. All he could hope for was that she continued to trust him.

Chapter 16

Ashford

Master demons didn't come on command. They came when they damn well pleased or if the situation presented a great opportunity. Ashford knew that better than anyone and hoped he had set the right mood for his former master. Lyla lay on the ground in a heap. The power drain had taken its toll on her. At one point, she had even fainted.

With a fissure of power, M'Kal stepped out of the portal. M'Kal looked like some sort of anime reject with his long blond hair done in a pointy and over dramatic fashion. He was tall and lithe yet extremely toned. A fact you couldn't help but notice since he dressed in tight leather pants and an open black button-up shirt. The vanity was real with this one.

Joining him were a couple of lackeys. Ashford remembered them always being around M'Kal. They were lesser demons, though, much less powerful than himself. Each one held a child in their arms. His children struggled and reached out for him as tears streamed down their little chubby cheeks.

"I hope you don't expect to lavish me with gifts and escape any kind of punishment. You have cost me greatly with your little escapade, and I intend to take that out of your flesh," M'Kal said with a sinister voice dripping in command even with its higher pitch.

Ashford gave a sheepish grin, bowing his head a bit. "My Lord, I apologize for the chaos this has caused, but my plan worked." Ashford looked up without raising his head, which gave a more wicked effect to his words.

"What the fuck are you talking about?" M'Kal seemed less than amused by Ashford's answer, but he wasn't to be deterred.

"I knew who guarded my children, and I knew if given the right atmosphere and opportunity I could seduce her. Unfortunately, it meant making sure everything was very real. There was no way I could have gotten her here for you any other way. Trust me, her power will be delicious and give you that boost you have been searching for over the last couple of centuries," Ashford explained.

"How dare you!" Lyla gasped, looking up at him with an expression of shock and betrayal.

The angel was too weak to do anything about it, so he didn't bother to acknowledge her. Instead, he stood up straighter so he could continue his conversation with M'Kal.

"So, are you telling me all of this was some sort of elaborate plot for you to get me more power?" M'Kal chuckled as he moved forward a little. "Very charming, but why would you bother to do that, and why should I even believe you?"

"You've had your sights set on taking out some of the other barons and growing your power structure. Let's be honest. The more power you have, the more power I have. I don't intend to be stuck in some shit job for the rest of my existence. When I saw the opportunity my children gave me to bring about your rise in power, I couldn't help myself." Ashford grinned even more, the expression reaching his eyes that blazed with energy.

"Oh, now, that is very clever. Between your little gift down there and your children, I believe we will be able to do just that. I still don't appreciate your tactics on this. You should have come to me about it." M'Kal sighed, a smile stretching over his lips. "But under the circumstances, I think your transgressions can be forgiven. I can at least ensure your punishment is less severe."

Ashford hadn't mentioned anything about his children, and hearing the baron's words did not sit well with him. However, he kept his strong resolve. "The children aren't ready for Hell yet. They need more time to develop. When they are ready, we can come back for them. It isn't like they are going to be protected now."

"We can't risk someone taking over their care.

Besides, I quite like the idea of having them around. They can learn young and become far more powerful than others of their kind. After all, they will have me mentoring them the entire time." M'Kal laughed loudly. Obviously, Ashford couldn't hide everything. "Surely, you didn't think I was going to leave them to you to take care of. I have more important things for you to deal with than changing diapers and reading books. Now, bring my present to me so we can be done with this wretched place."

Ashford knelt to pick up Lyla who squirmed and tried to get away. There was anger in her eyes, but her focus was on trying to get to the children despite her weakness. Damn, she sure did have heart. Before he could gather her in his arms, a bright flash of light radiated over the clearing. Zimarra sliced into the two lackey demons with her daggers, sending them falling to the ground. With a twirl and a flourish of power, she wrapped her wings around the twins before they hit the ground and teleported away with them.

M'Kal screamed in anger. He was enraged over the loss of the half-bloods and aggravated over the ambush of his lesser minions. Once Zimarra had taken the children to safety, Ashford manifested his swords, two twin falcata blades etched with demonic runes, and the edges of the forward curved weapons glowed like molten fire. They had been his weapons since his fall when he had lost the ones given to him by Heaven. He raised one up, standing over Lyla, ready to strike her.

"No, I want her alive when I consume her!" M'Kal yelled, darting in closer to interrupt his action.

Ashford ignored him, and his swinging downward blades whistled and left a dark-red trail of power in the air. The angel screamed and closed her eyes as the unholy weapons came down to hit and break the shackles that bound her wrists and power. Her body arched back, and she cried out from what he could only assume was a rush of her power returning to her, but he didn't have time to figure it out.

M'Kal realized what was going on, and the baron was not happy. With a flick of his outstretched hands, M'Kal summoned his own blade, Seraph Doom, a six-foot-long black blade that was almost two feet wide at the base and tapered down to a point. With a ragged edge, it flexed and moved like it was alive. On a closer look, it looked like an outstretched wing, because it was. He had ripped it off himself as he fell from Heaven. It had now been transformed into a weapon of living demon steel and one of the most powerful Ashford had ever seen.

Ashford's face turned white. He knew he was dead; he just needed to buy enough time for Lyla to get enough of her power back so she could escape to watch over his children, which was the second part of his plan. The first part had been accomplished when Zimarra had gotten his children safely away. It had taken a lot of effort to convince Zimarra to trust and help him. She had almost killed him when she had burst into the room after he had cuffed Lyla.

"Ashford, prepare for pain. I am going to cut off your limbs and slowly feed them to you." He sprinted forward swinging Seraph Doom with incredible force. Red hellfire swept around the edges of each feather. Ashford dodged backward, not even attempting to block. He almost made it, but the tip of his opponent's blade scored a long shallow slash across Ashford's stomach.

The lesser demon then went on the attack. He used his speed to his advantage, and his blades beat a staccato irregular rhythm against the larger slower blade. Trying to keep M'Kal from getting in any large attacks, Ashford spun and whirled, and tried   to dazzle his foe.

It worked for a while, but M'Kal was a very talented warrior. Soon, he adjusted to Ashford's attack pattern. He timed it and counterattacked with an empowered kick to his chest, blasting him back and to the ground. Ashford hit and rolled backward but was no longer on the offense. The more powerful demon streaked in using smaller more accurate cuts and thrusts Ashford could barely parry.

With his larger, heavier blade, M'Kal darted and slashed, mixing in kicks, all of which was backed by demon power. Still, the smaller demon blocked, dodged, and avoided all his former master's attacks. He was tiring though. Outmatched by a larger, stronger opponent. In desperation, Ashford feinted a swing toward M'Kal's head then swung low to score a minor hit on his leg. They battled back and forth, gaining and losing the advantage, while demon steel screeched and crashed together over and over in a flurry too fast for mortal eyes to see.

Despite being younger, smaller, and less powerful, Ashford started to gain the upper hand, scoring three more stinging attacks on his former boss. The blade in Ashford's hand snapped, the stress of blocking Seraph Doom too much, and the large demon blade sliced deep into Ashford's thigh.

M'Kal chuckled as Ashford crumpled to the ground. "I have changed my mind. You are too annoying to torture. I am going to just end you." He drew back his giant weapon to finish him. A flash of blue light exploded, blinding the demon baron and forcing a painful scream from him.

***

Lyla

Lyla had not come anywhere near to her full power, but she could not just lay there and watch the man she loved die. She flew forward and drove her small blades into M'Kal's torso.

Encountering his hidden body armor, her blades didn't do as much damage as she hoped.

"So, the bitch angel wants to play. Fine, it's been a long time since I was able to kill one of your kind." M'Kal swung at her with aggression, attempting to take her out fast.

She defended herself with her small weapons, and angelic and demonic energy flashed and crackled. If she had her full strength and was defending children, it would have been a difficult battle but possible to win. Since she wasn't, the fight did not last long. The demon baron shrugged off her offense and smashed through her defense, sending her to crumple onto the ground nearly defeated.

Wide-eyed, Lyla watched as M'Kal lifted his blade and brought it down to finish her. There was a joyous expression on his face a moment before he chopped down. Lyla braced herself for the finality that would come by his blade. A weight crashed into her body, and she looked down to see Ashford lying across her just as the sword slashed deep into his back. More joy covered the baron's face as he continued to sink the blade through flesh and bone. M'Kal looked down, and the look on his face turned to shock as he realized Ashford was lying across her.

An explosion of bright golden light knocked the demon lord backward. Lyla squinted through it, but the feeling of it was far more familiar than she had expected for the energy that usually came from her demon lover. Ashford's body rose above her, the light engulfing him and healing him. Wings spread free from his back, and he was encased in bright golden armor. Two blades manifested in his hands, and Lyla gasped as she saw Ashford in his full high angelic form. It was a beautiful sight, and it took her several breaths to recover from it.

Several feet away, M'Kal was also recovering. A venomous cry came from the demon lord as he raced toward them once more. Ashford did not waste time. He sprang forward and attacked with renewed vigor and power. It was a strength few angels possessed. Now it was a much more even fight as Ashford the warrior angel took on his former master. Angel and demon steel clashed and sang their dance of death. Neither opponent gained or lost ground for long.

That changed when Lyla threw herself into the battle. She, too, had been renewed and strengthened. Her chakrams had changed into axes, the circular blades now attached to brass handles giving them more striking power. She rushed into the fight, flanking M'Kal and slicing into him. They overwhelmed him, slicing, thrusting, and kicking until everything turned into a whirlwind of sparkling power and the music of war.

M'Kal could not fight them together, and panting, he backed away. "There will be a next time. Make no mistake about that," M'Kal said before he ripped open a portal and jumped in to disappear back to Hell.

Lyla stood there, not really sure what to say or do as she gazed upon Ashford in his new form. Never had she heard about a demon being returned to their angelic status, so this was all a bit shocking. The look on his face as he looked down at himself said he was just as surprised.

He rushed over to her and wrapped his arms around her, kissing her deeply. "Are you okay? I'm so sorry. I had to make it seem real so he would fall for the trap." Ashford's words came a mile a minute as he continued to hug and kiss her.

"I'm fine. How did you get Zimarra to help?" she asked, still trying to put everything into perspective.

"She came to the room having felt the power of the cuffs. She tried to kill me, but I explained my plan to her. She offered to help so long as I swore nothing would happen to you," Ashford answered, once again hugging and kissing her.

Finally, he pulled away and took a deep breath. He looked down at his blades, glancing over them for several long moments. "I lost these during the fall. I never thought to see them again. Of course, I never thought to be this again."

"Are you happy?" Lyla asked, not ready to let her guard down and get her hopes up.

"If I can be with you, then yes, I am the happiest man, er, uh, angel, who ever existed."

The next kiss was filled with even more passion and power than any before it. Every part of her burst with emotion as she clung to him. When they pulled away, she looked up into his eyes, still full of fire, only now they were golden. "I love you, Ashford."

"I love you too, my sweet Lyla."

Epilogue

Lyla

"Well, look at that. Your first write-up. I think we should frame it and put it on the wall," Zimarra joked while Lyla read over the message that had just come for her.

She was being reprimanded for working during her forced vacation. "This isn't funny!" Lyla protested, throwing the paper down on her desk.

"It's a little funny," Ashford chimed in from where he lounged in one of the chairs in their room.

After their fight with M'Kal, they had taken the children back to Becca. The children's mother had been overjoyed to see they were back in one piece and even more happy about the fact their father was no longer a demon. Explaining it had been a bit tricky. He now had regular visitation, which he savored with every fiber of his being.

Once the children had been returned to their mother, Ashford and Lyla had enjoyed the rest of the vacation together, sharing a room. They danced, played, and made love until they couldn't take much more, and then they would wake and do it all again. Lyla had never thought she would be so happy, and having Ashford with her did just that.

When they had returned to Heaven, Ashford had been summoned by the big man. Now he was part of the warrior ranks. While he still had a lot of loyalty to earn, he was starting to find his place.

"Well, I am not going to hang this on my wall. I don't care what either of you say." Lyla rolled her eyes and tossed something at Ashford. Her room was no longer sterile and perfect. Ashford's presence had brought about more color and comfort. She had hung pictures of the two of them and pictures of the children on the wall.

Due to her attachment with Ashford, the children had been assigned to another angel, something Lyla understood. "So, when do you leave?" Ashford asked, turning toward Zimarra.

Lyla's friend blushed a bit then sat down on the edge of the bed. "I'm not sure. I'm still planning. But I think it will be nice to have some time to myself. Not that I didn't enjoy our vacation, but after you joined in, I kinda felt like the third wheel."

"Sorry about that," Lyla said sheepishly.

"Don't be. I'm glad you found love as well as had so much fun. Now maybe you won't wait for all of eternity to go on another vacation. Who knows, maybe you can make a yearly trip to the resort," Zimarra suggested, wiggling her eyebrows, and Ashford chuckled. Zimarra got up to leave. "Well,

I will leave you two be. Have a nice night."

Once Zimarra was gone, Ashford walked over to Lyla. Her heart still skipped a beat when he approached her. Angelic power did not take away any of his sexiness. His arms wrapped around her, and he pulled her into him before his lips consumed her. When their lips parted, he spoke softly, keeping them close together. "She has a point. We will have to go out together more. I wouldn't mind going back another time."

"Maybe." Lyla licked her lips and looked up into his eyes. "Maybe we can go there after we get married."

A huge grin spread over his lips a moment before he kissed her again. This time, he ravished her, lifting her and carrying her the bed. They hadn't really talked about marriage, but Lyla had decided she was no longer going to be shy. If she wanted something, she was going for it. So, telling him that was her way of letting him know just where she saw their relationship going.

"I think I like the idea of that," Ashford answered before going back to making love to her. Yes, love. She loved him, cherished him. Having Ashford in her life had made her life whole.

About the Author

Cherron Riser was born in Dothan, Alabama on November 2, 1983. With her family being military, she spent a lot of her early childhood traveling all over the country, giving her a lot of new and different experiences, she would not otherwise have been given. When she turned ten, however, her family settled in the small town of Ozark, Alabama where she finished her high school career.

Today Cherron is a proud mother, sister, and daughter. She lives in a very busy house with her children and sister, and there is never a dull moment as they all enjoy taking on new adventures, going to Six Flags, and all things geeky.

All through her life, Cherron has been drawn to the arts. As a child, she danced and sang all the time, often driving her family crazy. During middle school, a group of friends and Cherron started "The Outcast" a club established for building a love of writing. Once the club was formed, Cherron was never seen without a spiral notebook and pen. She wrote daily, developing silly stories for her friends. After high school, Cherron began to write more serious stories and develop more original plot lines. It is a talent and love Cherron has developed over the years, filling her computer with story after story.

As an author, Cherron began her career as a self-published author, releasing the book Defying Destiny in March of 2015. She gives a lot of credit to her family and friends for inspiring her characters and worlds and looks forward to showing them to all her readers in the near future. Cherron can often be seen at conventions, both for readers and for geeks, as she is and will always be a geek herself, and proud of it.

More Works by Cherron Riser

Follow Cherron Riser

https://www.cherronriser.com/

Facebook –
https://www.facebook.com/CherronRiserAuthor/

Facebook Group-
https://www.facebook.com/groups/997158103671877/

Twitter – https://twitter.com/CherronRiser

Instagram – https://www.instagram.com/cherronriser/

Goodreads –
https://www.goodreads.com/author/show/8443066.Cherron_Riser

Newsletter –
https://landing.mailerlite.com/webforms/landing/g8y1j7?fbclid=IwAR1F2FbHVC-l6VKw3WPGVGN3HYu4EIKRSo_abywsJhZqSBcLDJidgcCCfh8

Nestled between Redemption and Damnation...

Crimson Moon Hideaway

Thank you for reading my contribution to the Crimson Moon Hideaway World! Reviews are greatly appreciated.

For more amazing stories in the Crimson Moon Hideaway World, follow us on Social Media:

Crimson Moon Hideaway website: https://www.blackhollowtown.com/crimsonmoonhideaway
Crimson Moon Hideaway Fan Page: https://www.facebook.com/groups/805037303324967
email: crimsonmoonhideaway@gmail.com

Merchandise is available for the Crimson Moon Hideaway World!

https://teespring.com/stores/crimsonmoonhideaway

Made in the USA
Columbia, SC
15 April 2022

58700107R10074